To The Beet

CATHLEEN ELLIS

v24-0307

YOUNG PEOPLE IN LOVE
IN THE HEARTLAND OF AMERICA

MONTANA

IOWA

COLORADO

KANSAS

GEORGIA

1

September 9, 2001

"Bobby John, thanks for meeting up. I gotta get a ride with Sheri in 10 minutes. She's closing up."

"Babydoll, when're we getting together again, my sexy sweetie?"

She stared, right into his dark blue eyes. They stood, the same height, next to his car. It was parked down the street, away from the cafe. He watched the streetlight catch in her pale blue, stunning eyes.

"It's over; I'm graduating in December, with all my AP stuff I'm almost a college sophomore, on to college."

"This's the first I've heard of all this."

"Yeah, that's right, you gotta get another chick to play with."

She tried with all her might to speak to him in a quiet melodic voice.

He attempted to touch her shoulder, but she stepped away from him. She shuddered, her mouth tasting vomit.

"You're the hottest, sweetest honey I've ever had. Right now you're stone cold as ice."

"Goodbye, Bobby John, hey I turn 16 tomorrow. And I got my whole life to live; I got no call to play the sex game we've had."

She gave him a soft smile, turned and walked away from him, back to the café where she worked 5 to 8 p.m. three nights a week.

She spoke out, "I'm done with him, my play toy."

A cold wind whirled around her as she made her way.

His eyes burned with tears as he thought back over that summer romance with her. He tasted vomit shooting up to his throat.

"She lied to me; I saw her ID indicating she was 18. She showed it to me. Lying, I didn't expect that, and all the drinking we did. Hey, I really cared about this little gal. Sheet, she's jail bait. And we had sex last night," he whispered. "I'm disgusted with myself."

His hand shook as he unlocked his car. On the way to his long-term hotel his whole body trembled; he had to pull over. Anger split his forehead with perspiration. Vomit roiled up into his throat again, burning the back of his tongue. He kept swallowing to keep it down.

∞

Tess kept a small smile on her face as she met Sheri at her car.

"It's over, Sheri, the booze, the sex. I had such a hold on his body. I loved the power; no regrets, mom shared some of her secrets about men, what they want and will do to get what they want."

She smiled, then a spasm of regret shook her, the losing him. Her fingers froze.

"I'm glad; you have school and your job. You don't want to do anything to jeopardize your great grades and college chances. And hey, Happy Birthday, your sweet 16th tomorrow."

Tess touched Sheri's shoulder before she got out.

"Thank you, you've been such a comfort for me. Marty, I mean Mom, well she's just into this new guy who hangs out."

"Tess, I care, your daddy cares, so does your Aunt Em."

"Thanks, I know I'm not alone, and I appreciate the ride home."

"You are so, so smart, Tess, so much going for you."

ℰℭ

"Happy Birthday to me, happy birthday to me," Tess sang as she got up the next morning, early, to clean up her mom's drinking mess from the night before. She started coffee, washed up the dishes and made order in the kitchen.

"At least the house will start out looking nice," Tess spat the words out.

She knew what the end of the day might bring. She took her coffee to her tiny bedroom, sipped some of it and then took a fast shower in the small bathroom next to her bedroom.

In the trailer house her mom rented there were two bathrooms, one next to her mom's bedroom at the other end of the trailer, and one for Tess. Next door to Tess was a little larger bedroom her mom used for her bookkeeping business. Marty worked from home, including payroll. Her mom's work hours stayed erratic. Some nights she worked all night, then slept in until noon the next day. The only thing Marty asked of Tess was to keep plenty of coffee made up, for whenever she woke up from her activities of the night before. Some days mom and daughter hardly saw each other.

"I'm off to school, Mom," she knocked on her mom's door.

"Have a good day, sweet girl," she heard her mom's groggy voice.

ℰℭ

Tess met her counselor, Mrs. Brendt, during her lunch break.

"I'm 16 today, September 10; I told mom I was off to school, and she said to have a good day, sweet girl."

"Oh, Tess," her counselor paused and Tess watched her forehead line with concern, "you OK with her not acknowledging your special day?"

"Used to it, Mrs. Brendt. I see dad tonight; he's got a car planned for me."

"I want you to have a good semester, Tess. We've worked together for two years now, planning how you're going to accomplish this, graduate early; then the move to Beet City, live with your Aunt Emily, and start college there. You've already been admitted to the community college?"

"That's right, and you've helped me apply for a grant to help with financial aid."

"And your Aunt Em?"

"She sees my ability, plans to help me with tuition, and I'll live with her; so she's taking care of my room and board."

"Wanted to ask you, what about health insurance?"

"Dad's gonna continue to cover me, all through college, and tuition help also. He saw how terrible, me getting so crosswise with his second wife, my stepmom. He did have full custody of me. And you know what happened at Dad's; I raised a lot of hell. And dad really had no choice but to ship me to my mom's. He really didn't want to do that. But he told me I'd learn to cope with my mom here in Farnon."

"It took you a while to change your ways, Tess. I remember what you were like when you came to Farnon High."

"Yeah," she raised her eyes to Mrs. Brendt, "My horrible mouth, I was a mess, complete and total. Oh, and I broke up with the older guy I had a fling with this summer, you know the lawyer who handles the law stuff on several beet exchanges in this area."

"And?"

"It was a really good thing that I did break up. I used a fake ID; he thought I was 18. I had serious power over him, a manipulative power, even though he's older and educated."

Mrs. Brendt swallowed hard and took a deep breath, in and out, before she spoke, "You have a good future, Tess."

"I do, and I gotta go. Thank you for being here for me, between you and my friend at work, Sheri, I really have a mother. I'm grateful for knowing you."

Her counselor heard the tremor in her voice, a gratefulness she hadn't expected.

"I'm here for you, Tess."

Tess nodded, smiling to her as she stood up.

"God bless and keep her," Mrs. Brendt whispered as Tess left her office.

ℰↃ

"Happy Birthday, sweet girl."

Tess filled with happiness at the sound of his voice, and his big smile to her.

"Dad, come in, I'll let mom know you're here to take me out. She's workin' in her office."

Tess tapped on her mom's office door.

"I'm going out with dad."

"Lemesee him for a minute."

Marty emerged from her office and followed her daughter down the short hall to the living room.

"Joe," she nodded to Tess's dad, "nice to see you; thanks for taking our sweet daughter out for her special day."

They gave each other a quick hug, stepped back and Marty returned to her daughter.

"They still take my breath away," he gazed at them and thought, "two of the most beautiful women I've ever seen."

He saw the curly black hair of each of the women, cut below chin length. But it was their eyes, Tess with pale baby blue, startling eyes, contrasting sharply with her dark hair. And Marty had more china blue eyes, still as stunning as her daughter's.

"You are your mom, Tess, more and more every day."

"Not," Marty interjected, "Tess is better looking, taller, slimmer, with a perfect figure. I'm getting a pudge in my middle," she giggled as she turned her eyes to Tess.

She patted her stomach, hidden by the long plaid shirt she wore.

"Ready?"

She nodded and waved bye to her mom.

Tess asked that they sit in a more private area of the restaurant. They ordered the meal, with a glass of wine for Joe, and a ginger ale for Tess.

"I have so much I want to say to you, Dad."

"Shoot."

Tess paused, tears coming to her eyes as she gazed to her dad.

"Want to apologize for my awful behavior and bad manners the last two years I lived with you. You married the lady who became my stepmom. I did not want to share you with anyone else. I wanted your love. It was my anger, like a fury; I acted out, it felt good to get that anger exposed. That was totally, absolutely uncalled for. No excuses, the anger eating me up, I coulda controlled that. But I decided not to. Please forgive me," she said the phrase slow, to emphasize it as her eyes implored her dad's face.

"The best thing you ever did was force me to live with mom. That's been some experience, but it helped me to start growing up. To sum up, I was an immature brat; everyone told me that. But I'm changing my ways.

First of all, I appreciate you carrying me on your health insurance for all this time. And you've said you'll continue to do that through college."

Joe gazed into his daughter's eyes, "That's correct. Tell me how all that's going."

"Admitted to Beet City's community college for spring semester. I'll graduate from high school at Christmas. I've taken a lot of AP classes and done real good. It's one place where I've channeled some of my anger, by having strong study habits, and good test-taking skills. Aunt Em's planning on me moving in at Christmas so I can start my classes in January."

"Excellent."

"Dad, because of my AP courses, I'll have most of my freshman year covered when I get to community college (cc). The cc accepted every single one of my AP classes, classes I'll not have to take 'cause I covered the college work in my high school class. Most important I tested well on the AP exams that I was required to take at the end of each one of the AP classes."

"So in the spring, will you finish up your first year?"

"Right, I'll have a whopping load," she nodded to her dad as their food arrived. "I'll be starting my sophomore classes this summer. With any luck I'll finish up, taking summer school and next fall." She looked at him and nodded, "I'll be able to start at the Wind River College, at junior status, after next Christmas."

"I am so proud of you, Tess, for all you've accomplished at Farnon High," he smiled and touched her shoulder. Tess noticed his shining eyes on her, warming her, clear to her toes.

After they finished their meal, they asked for decaf coffee to go with the chocolate cake for dessert.

"Aunt Em's paying for tuition, I'll help with that, and you'll stay with her?"

"Yes, with you continuing to cover me for health, like you said."

"And Tess, the car I'm giving you, to accomplish your degree, I'll help you with insurance and license plates/vehicle registration."

"I have so many people helping me. And I've just started using the moral compass you tried to teach me to have years ago. I was such a half-cocked jerk, so unappreciative."

A red burn of shame washed across her face and down her neck.

"You're being really hard on yourself, Tess. Good happened during your rough times, especially with you trying hard with your school work, taking on many extra classes. And your mom shared that lately you started helping around home. Plus you work three evenings a week. That's helpful for your time management skills, and giving you a little spending money."

"I save a little with each check I get, plus tips. But Dad, there was a long time where I lived without a conscience."

She sat for a little while without saying a word.

"I," she paused and decided it was time, "I met a man this summer."

"Older?"

"Yeah."

"Uh, divorced?"

"That's right, they split after five years; he wanted kids. Seemed they couldn't have any. Both got tested, he had a low sperm count. He was rebound, and I wanted a fling."

"What about your age, what did he say?"

"I lied, used a fake ID, to drink, to convince him he needed to move on."

She watched as her dad's lips thinned, "Protection?"

"Uh huh, condom, but with his low sperm count."

"You never know."

"I split with him, and I finally told him how old I really was. I think I scared the buggers outa him. Hey, he's a lawyer."

"Oh, Tess."

His sky-blue eyes pierced hers.

"Another half cup?"

"Yes, thanks, then you gotta get me home; you got 45 minutes to your home."

They drank their coffee. It was silent as he drove her home. He walked her to the front door of the trailer. She got out her key. They hugged.

"Dad, I love you. I am a child of God, but so are you and everyone else."

"I love you, sweet girl."

He kissed her on her forehead.

"I'll get in touch with you about the car."

She nodded, turned and unlocked the door. She turned back to see him get in his car.

He saw her wave to him and then she blew him a kiss.

ॐ

Tess saw the empty space where Marty parked her car.

"She may be away 'til morning," Tess decided, "the new guy," she shook her head.

She went straight to her room to finish up her homework. She took out her calendar to see which days she worked. It looked like Wednesday through Friday of this week. Then she slept until her alarm the next morning.

She made coffee, cleaned up the kitchen, and showered. And her mom had not come home, no phone call. There were fewer kids on the bus today, as sometimes happened. When she got to her high school, teachers stood in front of their classroom doors, letting students know there was an assembly all needed to attend. Teachers accompanied their respective students to the gym and sat with their class.

They watched TV monitors for 15 minutes after they learned of the news. Students cried, prayed, and spoke in quiet tones.

Along with the rest of the student body, Tess stumbled through her day, not really comprehending what happened in the eastern part of her country. She rode the bus home and sat in front of the TV as the news kept looping around the enormous tragedy that occurred that morning. She made coffee, drank some and went to her room to study. On her CD player she put on a *Cold Play* album. And she heard from Sheri. At Sheri's church there would be a prayer service. Tess raced through her homework, had a sandwich, and met Sheri at the entrance to the trailer park.

"Your mom?"

"She's been gone since last night. Dad and I did my birthday dinner, and when I got home mom was gone. She never leaves a note."

"Yeah, that's your mom."

They sat with the congregation and many visitors jammed together in the small Farnon Community Church. Tess heard folks openly sobbing and whispering prayers before the service began. The minister, Reverend Dawson, kept the message short, asking all to pray for those impacted by the tragedies of the Twin Towers, the Pentagon, and the field in Pennsylvania. Special prayers went out for the aunt of one of the congregation members. She worked in the Twin Towers, and the family had no word from her.

The mourners sang, with their hymn books, and without any music accompaniment. The service ended, but people did not get up and leave. Almost everyone stayed, too saddened to even move for a time.

"What if that was me?" Tess kept asking herself as she sat there. "One of those who died; that would'a been bad for me. I'm right now cleaning up the mess I've made. What am I to take from this? Faith, so many folks have faith in me, to take control of my life, to make it a good life. And hope, reverend talked about hope. I now have some hope; I can see clear what I must do, my path. My family, they have hope in me. And where has love been? I know dad loves me, and Aunt Em. I must love, me, myself, God, love God, and love my family, yeah, even my mom, and, uh huh, Bobby John, I hope he finds love in his life. Mom has tried; I think I kinda get that now. Oh my gosh, to have me dumped on her when I was behaving so horrible. Amends, Tess, you got amends to make. Yeah, this is my second chance. Thank you, God, for my life. Please forgive me."

She gazed ahead, the images of the day bombarding her brain. The vomiting tickle in her throat did not go away. The only thing that helped her, continuing prayer. Sheri touched her shoulder.

Tess nodded; they rose together and left the pew in the church. Outside folks cried and hugged each other and prayed aloud. She thanked Sheri for the ride. She smelled coffee brewing as she came into the living room of her mom's home. The loud TV kept up the news reports which she watched for a little while after she and her mom hugged.

"God bless our country; I, I just feel so helpless," her mom whispered to her as they hugged.

Tess knew she was too jumpy to go to bed. She did a load of wash and washed and dried the pans that did not go in the dishwasher. After that she dried the clothes and distributed them out to her and her mom. She kept returning to the TV, now turned down several decibels as the news reports kept being more and more grim.

"Mom," she knocked on her mom's office door, "I'm headed for bed. And I need another hug."

As they hugged, Tess spoke out, "Mom, when you leave, scribble me a note, leave it on the dining room table. I really want to know where you are, and that you're OK. I'll do the same, just for this next while, until I leave at Christmas."

As they stepped back from each other, Marty nodded, "I agree that is a very good idea, sweet girl."

"I love you, Mom."

Marty nodded to her daughter, with tears in her eyes. Tess watched her mom pat her heart three times.

"Please call your dad and Aunt Em."

"I will."

ॐ

Tess heard quiet in the halls at school. The shock of what happened affected the high school students, in a different way from littler kids. She never saw so many students pray, in class, in the halls, comforting each other.

The pep assembly Friday morning, planned to cheer on the football team that night, turned into a time of prayer, with coach talking only briefly about the game. The school playing Farnon High decided the best thing for everyone was to go on with the game, to pray, but for students and everyone else to move on with their lives.

Tess worked at her fastest pace that Friday night. Folks arrived to eat before the football game started. The talk at all the tables revolved around folks getting on with their lives, after the horrors of Tuesday. In the conversations she heard as she served customers they wanted the football game to be played. And they wanted life to continue as it had before.

"No travel by airplane, how long will that be?"

She heard that again and again. But she knew that airports could not open until travelers felt secure in flying. Many people talked of traveling long distances, just doing it by car. It took longer, but the safety issue, that was a big deal.

By 8 p.m. Tess felt exhaustion creep into her bones, making her light-headed. Shortly before she left the café she did have a hamburger and fries. The owner always made her eat, for free, at the end of her shift. She rode her bike home. She hummed, too tired to sing out. "Be Still My Soul" is what she hummed. It was one of the songs from the Tuesday night prayer meeting. She looked up at the sky seeing several stars just peek out.

"At least you're still up there, you stars. You're one thing remaining the same," she choked as tears came to her eyes.

She reviewed her homework situation in her head. Saturday she would get all the work done. Sunday her dad would bring the car and have her practice driving in the sedan he wanted her to have.

₧

People at school did not recognize her. That's because this fall she changed the clothes she wore, improved her manners, and tried to smile more.

"You're different, Tess."

"Yeah, Matt, that's what has to happen."

She sat in the lunch room on Monday, having her sack lunch from home, with milk she bought in the lunch line. Matt and she joined up the middle of last year at lunch. Neither one had friends. Both were super smart, freaky; kids that the other students shied away from.

"What about joining National Honor Society?"

"Matt, you should. And yeah, I'm smart, but, you gotta know this, I'll have enough credits at Christmas, semester's end, to graduate. So I'm moving on to the cc in Beet City. Please, you join, OK?"

"Hey, you're just telling me this stuff. Was it 9/11, did that help you make up your mind?"

"A little bit, but this change's been comin' for a while. Now I've finalized everything. And dad brought me a car on Sunday; I got to practice drive. Mom says she'll help me with that, the practice driving with another adult. So this fall I gotta practice, study for my written and actual driving exams, then get my driver's license."

"I got mine, but I gotta pay for my gas, insurance, and plates on my car. So that's why I work late days and all day Saturdays at my uncle's auto shop, learning how to fix cars."

She smiled to him, "Like my dad says, a good mechanic is worth his weight in gold."

"Yeah, well, that'll come; I just gotta keep learning everything I can."

"You need to get your high school diploma."

"I understand that completely; one day, maybe I'll do what you're doing, go to the cc, take auto mechanics and get some kind of certification."

"You'll make more money that way."

"Right."

"See ya."

Tess nodded and gave him her bright smile as she got up. She had a few minutes so headed for the library to study.

That afternoon her last class was chorus and her teacher asked her to stay for a minute as class let out. Once the students filed out, she went to her teacher.

"Miss Chalmer, what's up?"

"Two things, Tess, first, Mrs. Brendt talked to me about you, leaving at the end of the semester."

"Right, graduating early."

"May I encourage you, to continue singing, wherever you can, in a church choir where you're moving to, or if your school has some kind of choral group. Your voice is so absolutely marvelous. And you've not had vocal coaching."

"I'll think about that; I'm anxious to get my cc courses out of the way, to move on to Wind River College, there in Beet City."

"You really are interested in graduating from college."

She looked into Miss Chalmer's eyes and nodded, "I am," and then she paused, "Elementary education, working with young ones and hoping to help with a vocal program at whatever school I'll end up at, so I plan to take several music classes."

"Wow, an awesome goal, Tess," her teacher nodded to her. "And second, I have to admit, your appearance, so dramatically changed. You are very beautiful, but no one knew that, until your new clothes, your new way of wearing your hair, showing off your marvelous eyes."

"That was one of my summer goals, to work enough at the café to buy outfits for school, skirts, tops, tights, summer and winter, with the idea that I was college-bound. It's gonna happen, and I am so excited."

"I've written a letter of reference for you, at Mrs. Brendt's request, to go along with the grant application to help you at the cc in Beet City."

"Thank you."

"Tess, have your AP teachers done the same thing?"

"Yes, I believe they have; anyway, I requested their help. I can tell you they were surprised I was moving on."

"Right, so soon."

"Thank you, Miss Chalmer, you're very encouraging and helpful to me. And you know how much I love your class, love to sing. I gotta jet, or I'll miss the bus."

"Yes, go, I'm sorry to keep you."

Tess smiled to her, "That's OK, I loved what you had to say."

As she climbed on the bus, she tried to count how many more times she would ride this school bus, before the holidays.

"And never again," she whispered.

"But winter will come," she thought, "and I'll have to figure out how to get to my cc classes. Aunt Em, she'll know about buses. Hey, different community, different school, I gotta adjust, wherever I am. Oh yeah, I'll have my car, but with the winter weather here in Montana, I've got to have an alternative transportation."

8

She sat with her mom the next Saturday afternoon, before she headed out for a football game Tess could actually attend.

Most of the games occurred on Friday nights; she always worked Fridays.

"Mom, please, I need you to commit to my practice driving for the next six weeks."

"Sunday mornings, for an hour, then I'll go to church with you. I noticed you're attending, with Sheri."

"Uh huh, I like the reverend there; his sermons make good sense. At least I understand what he's saying."

"Good, maybe I'll even go after you can drive by yourself."

"It would give us a little time together."

Marty turned to her daughter, "I looked at my calendar for the rest of this year. There aren't going to be many more times that we'll be together. Then you'll belong to the world."

They hugged, and then started crying.

"I love you, Mom."

"And I love you, Tess."

ॐ

"I'm inviting you to come to the Homecoming Dance with me."

"Matt, like, are you asking me out on a date?"

He watched her eyes, surprised, blinking.

"I am; you're leaving."

"Right."

She paused and smiled to him from across the lunch table, "Thanks, that sounds like fun. I accept."

"Have you ever been to Homecoming Dance?"

"Nope, no dance, no prom, I kinda've missed out on high school stuff."

"So, we'll make up for those missed dances," he nodded and gave her his wide smile.

ॐ

Sheri helped Tess with a dress, a dark red one, something Sheri had in the back of her closet, that didn't fit her anymore. Sheri made the top part of the dress a little smaller by taking in the sides.

"The full skirt of the dress will be perfect for dancing, Tess," Sheri smiled to her. Then Tess tried the dress on in the café bathroom. She slipped out and waved to Sheri.

"It's perfect, thank you, Sheri."

"Yes, it fits fine, from me to you."

Tess helped Sheri close up the café. The manager left a little early to attend the Homecoming game that Friday night.

"Tomorrow night, with a nice guy, a beautiful dress, my one-time high school dance."

Sheri drove her home and patted her shoulder as Tess got out with her pretty dress, "Have a wonderful time."

"That's thanks to you, special friend."

Marty's car was gone. But Tess saw a note on the dining room table.

She whispered as she read it out loud.

"See you tomorrow afternoon. I'll want to see you in your special dress, Tess. Love, Mom"

"Thank you God, it's working, we're getting better at communicating."

Tess rose early the next morning and started on her homework. Her mom promised her a driving time on Sunday morning, an hour before church. So far that was working for Tess and her mom. Tess only had a few more hours of driving time before she qualified to take her exams. Whenever they went out together Tess drove and Marty shared what she could of driving lessons for her daughter.

Tess looked up from her homework and checked the clock.

"Just a half hour left of work; let me look outside."

Tess put on her sweatshirt and walked around the mobile home. She saw grass of all lengths, ugly, with a few leaves from the maple tree in the back. She tried to remember when she mowed last. Then she shook her head.

"I'll fix this."

She proceeded to start the lawn mower after she took it from their small storage shed behind the trailer. After she mowed, she raked up and bagged the clippings and leaves and walked them to the large trash container used by the tenants in this row of mobile homes.

It looked like her mom tried to grow flowers in a pot on the landing of the front porch steps.

"No follow through, that's my fault, I coulda watered these."

Once she fixed that damage she stepped out on the asphalt street that ran between the rows of homes.

"Looks better, I'll water a little, then get in to finish my homework. Actually I'm embarrassed for Matt to see this shabbiness. Just a little effort, hey, good job, Tess."

She smiled to herself as she thought of her Aunt Em and what all she could do to help her aunt while she lived there.

$\wp$

"Like the DJ?"

"Yeah, Matt, he's good. The stuff he plays is pretty easy to dance to. And you look amazing. A professional haircut does wonders for your face."

"Think I'm capable of becoming a handsome guy?"

"You already are, dude. I've seen a couple young ladies give you several looks. I know they're not sure who you are. Uh," she paused, "you look so different."

"Hey, and so do you. Some guys have checked you out, same deal, they're not sure exactly who you are."

They danced and danced, having fun, taking a break and getting punch and cookies. A senior asked Tess to dance. He asked her who she was because he wasn't sure. She told him, and he acted surprised.

"I'm mostly in AP classes."

"That's why, I don't have classes with you. And uh, do you work at the café on Main Street?"

"I do, after school, several nights a week."

"Hey, I enjoyed the dance, take care."

"You also."

She smiled to him as he took her back to where Matt stood.

"He didn't know who I was, for sure."

"Well, you're different from the old days lunch room look."
They laughed together as they nodded.

"It was fun, the dancing and conversation; you're helping me learn to be more sociable, thanks," she looked to him as they walked to her home.

"I had a good time with you, Tess, uh, what about your wheels?" he asked as he saw a second car parked in their driveway.

"Yeah, driving soon."

"Good luck."

He kissed her on her cheek and walked down the steps and back to his car.

He watched her wave to him and smile. He nodded.

⃝

"How many weeks?"

"Three, I'm getting so excited."

Tess nodded and smiled. She looked around the table at her family.

"So unbelievable," she thought as she gazed at her family members.

Her mom invited her dad, his wife, Angela, her grown son, Todd, and her granddad on her dad's side to Thanksgiving dinner. For now it might be a last time Tess would see her parents together. The meal celebrated Tess, for her hard work, graduating soon, now knowing she had a grant to help her with her classes at the Beet City cc.

And it gave Tess occasion to wonder about her dad as they sat eating. His blonde hair and sky-blue eyes contrasted to his own dad's black hair and dark brown eyes. And her Aunt Em, dad's younger sister, she had the same dark hair and eyes. Her dad and aunt looked nothing alike. Genetics were sorta strange, she decided.

"Someday I'm gonna ask Granddad Jack. I remember grandma having dark brown eyes, can't remember her hair color, it kept changing, depending on the year. Reddish was her hair color the year she died. I wonder, can two brown-eyed parents have a child with eyes as blue as dad's?"

"Dinner, delicious, Marty, and I know Tess helped," her granddad commented as they completed Thanksgiving dinner.

Marty decided on ham. And Tess agreed that there was less prep work with it. The two of them fixed up potatoes, salad, rolls, and pumpkin pie for dessert. Joe brought a small relish tray of carrots, celery, broccoli and cherry tomatoes. No one had to slave in the kitchen for hours ahead of time.

Tess learned many tips from working at the café, about cooking and getting a meal ready in quick order. She passed those on to Marty that fall. It helped them improve their cooking and baking techniques. For both of them cooking became an easier process.

"Girls cooked; guys clean up," Jack announced. "We'll have pie a little later, OK?"

Everyone agreed. The gals sat in the living room with their coffee, keeping an eye on the football game they turned on after the meal concluded.

"You are beautiful, Tess, your hair, outfit, so nice, what a wonderful change."

"Thanks, Angela, Mom and I went to a hair salon in the summer. The beautician really knew what to do with our curly black hair and shape of our faces. It's all in the cut of it."

"All we gotta do is keep the haircut up before it gets too long. There's a real trick with naturally curly hair."

Tess looked from Angela to her mom, "A couple minutes extra with a curling iron, that's what it takes."

"Is your Aunt Em ready for you?"

"Right, Mom and I visited her last weekend. She couldn't come for Thanksgiving here, so we went to her, took her pumpkin bars."

Marty nodded, "Which she really appreciated and ate with great gusto. It looks like Tess will do the cooking when she gets there at Christmas."

"Your aunt, Joe's sister, not a cook?"

"Apparently not; looks like she kinda lives on dinners from the grocery store freezer."

"She devotes so much time to her students and she puts in an hour at the end of the day working in the school's library, uh, the media center, is what they call it now," Marty added.

"Yeah, teachers at Emily's elementary school staff the library; there's no dedicated person for the library."

"Money?"

"Always," Tess nodded to Angela.

Marty looked to her daughter, "It'll face you, Tess, when you get to your school to work with little children."

"That's right, I'll have extra duties. That's just the way things are; we learn to make do with what's given to us."

"And you know what you'll want, for extra duty."

"Absolutely, anything to do with music, the special programs at Christmas and in the spring."

"You mean there won't be a music teacher at your school?"

Tess nodded to Angela, "Possible sharing, of a teacher, between several different schools. Often now, they're not dedicated, especially art and music, teachers for one school alone.

"It's been so long ago, with Todd."

Marty looked to the women, "School finance, it's a different beast than it was years past."

"You get into that a little bit, with your payroll and accounting business, right?"

"I do, Angela, making ends meet is kinda universal, across all finance structures."

"Unbelievable, how well that went," Tess thought after they all had the pie, declaring it very delicious.

Then the group departed; her granddad back to spend the night with Joe, Todd and Angela. Marty went to lie down. She would spend this night with Tess but planned to be with her guy for Saturday night.

ℰ

The next Tuesday morning Tess scheduled her driving test at the DMV. She also would take the written exam. Marty seemed almost as excited as Tess was to get her license.

"She won't have to cart me around anymore," Tess thought about that as she continued to study, her school work, and her license.

And the day came when she got her license.

"On my own, oh wow, hey, ease up, girl, freedom, oh my gosh,"

Tess nodded her head as she drove herself home from the café. In two weeks she would take finals, and sail away to a new life in a new world.

She called Bobby John after she got home from her shift.

"Can I meet you?"

"Absolutely, tell me where and when."

An early evening found Tess ordering a soda, and Bobby John had a beer. It was the bar where they often met the summer before.

"I heard some urgency in your voice, Tess, what's up?"

"First, thanks for meeting me so quick. It's been a good while."

"I love you, babe."

Tess nodded to him as they sat across from each other in a corner of the bar, away from the spot where they always sat before.

"I'm having a baby. It's yours; there has been no other man."

"A baby, I, I," he paused, took some deep breaths, and shook his head, "all this time I thought I couldn't, never would have a kid."

Tess continued to watch his eyes, to see his reaction.

"I'll marry you right now; our child needs both parents."

"Whoa up, buster," Tess shook her head, seeing his happy face.

He watched her somber look, her lips thin, unsmiling.

"You're keeping it?"

"I am, this child is a gift from God. I have responsibilities, to myself, and to you."

"Unbelievable, never thought I would have a child, in this way. Babe, used condoms."

"I know we did," she nodded.

"I have a responsibility to this child, Tess. I promise I will carry health insurance on this child and provide child support. I've seen what happens when a child isn't cared for, for God's sake, I'm a lawyer."

They sat, saying nothing, just listening to a song coming from the guitarist who played some nights at this bar.

"What about school, oh, Tess, you'll go on, right?"

He tried to smile to her, but could not.

"Of course, in time I'll be an elementary school teacher."

"I will help make sure that happens; my child, with a mom who is a teacher. That will be a wonderful thing."

He watched her shake her head, "I will not marry you; I don't love you. Someday I will find that one special guy, but not now. I got big responsibilities, big challenges ahead."

"What about your Aunt Em?"

"She's on board, will help me with the child. As a teacher she gets summers off, that'll help with my going to school all year round."

"Tess, I plan to pay for the child's care, child care, and later child support."

"Wow, you're being especially generous."

"The baby is my child, too," he nodded his head. "You'll absolutely keep me in the loop, ultrasound pictures."

"No ultrasound pictures, just the doc will see those; I don't want to know if it's a boy or girl, until birth."

"You are taking responsibility for what's happened."

"I am, Bobby John, and so are you. We'll see about your follow through 'cause you've just pledged thousands and thousands of dollars to care for this child over the next years."

"I'm taking responsibility for what's happened. It's hard to believe you are just 16; there's been some maturity happening over the past months for you."

"Yeah, pretty fast. She shook her head, "being a liar isn't sitting too well with me now. God and I have a relationship. My relationship will remain with Him, for the rest of my life."

"What about your mom?"

"On board, she was 17 when I was born. Mom and Dad decided to marry. They later regretted that. I've been really lucky, no morning sickness, just super tired at night, especially after my café shift. But I'm quitting after next week. I'm tall, think I'll carry the baby pretty much within; maybe I won't show for a long time. I need to get this next semester completed; it'll be my toughest one 'cause I'm gonna carry extra hours. All I'll have to do is study; should be very doable. And of course, help Aunt Em. I can cook and housekeep. I'm doing a lot of that now."

"You have been, since you were a little girl."

"Yeah, I really helped dad, until he married Angela and she moved in with us."

"You took good care of your dad."

"I did, and when she came, I just lost it, my anger, rage; how could my dad care about anybody but me?"

He heard the loudness of her voice.

"You've learned to love others, besides your dad, even caring maybe just a little bit for your mom?"

He finally saw her smile.

"Yeah, it's better with my mom than it's ever been. I'm growing up, Bobby John."

"Ready to face the world of much higher education?"

"Uh, huh, cc is much higher education?"

"It is."

They walked out together to her car.

"Be safe, getting home, you have a precious one to think about now."

"I do."

He kissed her forehead. They hugged.

"God bless and keep you both, Tess."

ℰↃ

"I'm graduated; start after the first at the cc."

"Thank you for your call, congratulations on finishing up, awesome, as you planned. I needed to tell you when we met a few weeks ago, you looked so wonderful, a pink in your cheeks I've not seen before."

"Thanks and I have other news."

"Tell me."

"Bobby John, early June, that's the babe's birth time."

Tess felt a jolt all through her body as she heard his gasp. He cried, into the phone, unable to say a word to her. "I, I still can't believe this is happening, uh didn't have any idea of your due date." He paused, "Yeah, that's nine months since the start of school."

"After two terms I'll be at Wind River College."

"You're gonna jam everything into that time frame, at the cc?"

"Right, after that, three hard semesters at Wind River, then student teaching my final term."

"Grade you'd really like to do?"

"Students in third grade, remember I know somethin' about kids. I will keep you in the loop as baby grows and my school completion date nears."

"I know you will; this is my child, Tess. When do you move?"

"Tomorrow, that's why I needed to talk to you. You spend most of your time at the beet exchange in Brickville now. We've got each other's phones and e-mails. That's how we'll stay in touch, like our cell now."

"I'm very proud of you, Tess. Our baby is in good hands."

"Hey, I got experience, yeah two summers, at 13 and 14, I took care of two different families of four kids, a baby in each one. They were families in our trailer park."

"Did you like it, uh, the work with kids?"

"Absolutely, the kids were my helpers, 8 to 5, five days a week. Except for the baby in each family, the kids had library cards. And we had several reading times every day. Mom helped me take them to the library once a week. And with Mom's help we went to the community swimming pool a couple of times for swimming lessons. I just considered the kids my own. So yeah, I got experience, and yeah, two kids in each family really took to swimming. That's thanks to me."

"You must be proud; it's definitely one thing you never shared with me."

"It was one of my proudest times, to know that those kids had the ability to save themselves in a water emergency."

It was quiet for a moment, "We're all in God's hands."

"In God's hands, yes, you and I both are Tess, and so is the child you carry. Please, have a happy Christmas."

2

"Ten days, I have ten days to get my new life in order," she whispered, "and to have a happy Christmas."

Aunt Em still had more time with her students before her holiday break. Tess brought in all her possessions. She got everything in her car, the important items of her life, from her mom's trailer. She set them in a corner of Emily's living room. She danced around in this living room, singing out the words to "Silent Night." Tess took a look at the bedroom where she would be staying for the next few years.

"Pale green, I know Aunt Em will approve," she spoke at the doorway to the bedroom.

Tess made herself a sandwich and then went to the paint store for paint and supplies. Aunt Em asked her to find a small Christmas tree. She did that at the lot near the store. She returned with her goodies, the tree a Douglas fir, 4 ½ feet tall. She inhaled its woodsy fragrance as she brought it in the home. By late afternoon she painted the small bedroom and started to decorate the tree. Earlier, Emily set out the ornaments she wanted on the tree, and where she wanted the tree in the room.

Tess stopped her tree decorating in the living room to put her bedroom back in order, to vacuum and put all her stuff there. The bedsheets, pillow cases, and bedspread all needed washing. Tess started in on that chore. Back she went to the tree decorating.

"How long since I've eaten? I'm really hungry," she spoke out.

She drank milk and had a cookie. Then she began fixing hamburgers and fries for dinner.

"Aunt Em will appreciate this," Tess looked around at her efforts, the dinner nearly finished, the tree decorated, and her room starting to look like her very own bedroom. The rehung drapes matched the clean bedspread and sheets she put back on the bed.

"The room color, so nice, and so much cleaner," she nodded.

Tess peeked into the larger of the guest bedrooms. When she and her mom came to visit before Thanksgiving they helped move one of the single beds from the room that would become Tess's bedroom to the room that was to be baby's room. With the single bed set along one wall, acting like a day bed, the room still had space for a baby bed, changing table, and a small two drawer dresser. Tess could imagine how all that would look, even though she would need to locate the baby gear.

When she and her mom came to Emily's, they painted the walls of the baby's room a very pale yellow. Tess smiled as she stood in the room.

"I just don't feel pregnant; please, Lord, keep me in good health. I'll see my new ob/gyn in the next few days. Dad, thank you for covering me on your insurance until I'm graduated. Then Bobby John says he'll help out with baby's insurance," she spoke out.

She exhaled a deep breath, "We'll see."

℘

"Everyone, this is my niece, Tess. She's living with me, for several years, going to school. Then she'll be a fellow teacher, hoping for upper elementary."

Tess heard clapping all around.   Emily invited Tess to the Christmas Eve luncheon, a tradition that teachers in her school kept up for many years. About a third of the group was single, including two men, the rest married or divorced.

Through the delicious potluck Tess took the opportunity to meet as many of the faculty as she could. She asked them what it was like to be a mentor teacher to student teachers in the elementary education program at Wind River, the college in their Beet City community. Nearly all of them got a chance to be mentor teachers.   Student teachers desired Emily's elementary school as their location for their internship. Oaktrail Elementary got top notch ratings, and the teachers really cared about children. Tess saw that in all of Emily's actions, from the time Tess first met her aunt as a young child.

"Aunt Em, thank you for inviting me. I learned a bunch, just talking to those talented folks you work with."

They walked down the street, from the principal's home to the sedan Tess now drove. A small snow squall occurred the evening before.

"A white Christmas, Tess, that's so wonderful to have snow on the ground. We were beginning to wonder about the lack of snow for this time of the year."

"Wonder no more," Tess turned to her aunt and smiled.

ℂ

When they got home, Tess made the two pumpkin pies they would donate to the city's Food Pantry for the noon Christmas dinner.   They got ready for the First Community Church's 7 p.m. Christmas Eve service. Emily sang in the choir. Tess sat in a pew near the front of the church. She wanted to hear the choir, and more important, what reverend had to say.

The choir director found Emily as she put on her choir gown.

"Em, our lead singer, she's got laryngitis she can't shake. What are we gonna do; we're short several people who are away for the holidays?"

Emily nodded her head, "Let me ask my niece; she's starting community college in a few days. She has an incredible voice, been singing in her school's choir for the past year and a half."

"You'd mentioned that to me; that's why I came to you, wasn't sure she'd moved to Beet City yet."

Emily found Tess and asked her to step into the aisle.

"We need your singing voice; someone got sick in the choir, can you help?"

"I'll try, I may not know the song, but usually I can figure it out by part way through the first verse."

Tess followed Emily to the choir room which the choir shared with the minister, deacons and whoever helped with that service. A choir member found Emily one of the green robes the whole group wore. Another person showed her the songs they would sing. Tess stepped away from the group to look at the four songs they would sing, one before, two during, and one at the end of the service. She studied the music and lyrics in the several minutes before the service would begin.

She returned to the choir leader. The woman watched the smile and glorious blue eyes of this beautiful young woman who nodded to her.

"Yes, I can help. There's only one song I'm not certain about. I'll just blend in with all of you, in a soft voice until I'm sure I've got the words matched with the music."

⁊⊃

Tess marveled at the choir's singing, the melodic voices, and hearing the minister's holiday message. She couldn't believe the quickness of the service. She watched a happy crowd mill around in the room where the choir hung up their robes.

"Merry Christmas, oh Merry Christmas," she heard as she passed that greeting to other members of the group.

"Thank you for singing with us, what a melodious voice you have," a choir member patted Tess's arm and nodded to her.

"Oh Aunt Em, it was wonderful to sing, to worship in the special way the singers do," she turned to her aunt as they walked along the sidewalk outside the church to Emily's car.

"Maybe you'd like to sing until babe comes?"

"I'd like that very much; Sunday mornings," she paused, "I'll get up early to study anyway. Choir practice, it's before service?"

"Yes, a half hour before, we use the piano in the choir room to practice."

ଔ

Tess gazed around at the crowded hall where those who needed Christmas dinners gathered.

"And I thought I had it rough, but I always had enough food to eat."

It sobered her to see the number of children who ate the dinner. She wondered to herself what they ate, especially during this holiday time. There were no breakfasts, or hot lunches, because the schools closed.

"Aunt Emily," Tess asked as they cleaned off the tables, pulled chairs away, and swept the floors after the dinner, "what do these youngsters eat, during this time, before school starts again in the new year?"

Her aunt stood close to her and spoke in quiet tones, "Parents come here, to the Food Pantry, to pick up what food is available. It's near the end of the month, so the pantry food supply gets lower, especially this holiday time."

"And the parents may not get paid until the end of the month."

"Yeah, a paycheck so they can go to the store for food."

Tess paused, "Oh my gosh, I cannot imagine, what do they eat?"

"Cereal, mostly with part milk and part water; noodles, with cheese is a highlight."

"So you see this first hand."

"Yes, at least a third of my students have parents who use food stamps."

"So those youngsters, they probably also get the reduced rates or free for breakfast and lunch at school?"

"Yes, Tess."

Tess saw the shake of her aunt's head and the sad glint in her eyes.

"Help, little kids need help; I just now know what it must be like for them walking into school, hungry."

"One day, you will be more than just a teacher with the young ones you'll work with."

She gazed at her aunt as they got ready to leave the pantry, "Be more than just a teacher," she whispered.

℘

Late Christmas afternoon, after Emily and Tess opened presents Tess called and spoke to her parents.

"Helping at the Food Pantry, singing in the church choir, those are special projects for you, Tess. I'm proud of you for those efforts."

That's what her parents told her in those holiday calls.

"I'm shedding my anger, Dad, replacing it with efforts I can make to help. I feel like a so much better person."

"Good for you, Tess, Angela sends along her holiday best wishes."

"And thank her, you also, for the gift certificate, stuff for baby."

"You're welcome, good luck with your next semester."

℘

Tess looked up at the clock on the cc's library wall that spring semester.

"Five minutes, I gotta leave in five," she whispered.

Craig Huntcrowe gazed at Tess from where he sat three chairs down and on the other side of the table from her.

"On Thursday, when I come here between classes, I'm gonna sit down next to her and introduce myself. Those eyes, magical, blue, enchanting. I want to know, at least her name. Course, that's if she sits here," he thought.

February snows melted into warmer March days as Tess trudged through her time in lectures and homework. She returned to her study place in the library as many times during the day as she could to study and prep for exams. At 5:15 each afternoon she left for home. Tess found several of her classes interesting and others she knew she had to have to transfer to Wind River.

She received essential help from a transfer evaluator in the Records and Registration Office at the cc. That woman knew the transfer evaluators at Wind River College, and they all worked together. The goal remained for a community college student to have as many credits as possible that would transfer to the student's program of study at Wind River.

Tess felt blessed that she knew Grace at the cc, and that Grace worked close with Wendy, the transfer evaluator at Wind River. She also talked with the woman in charge of teacher certification at the college. As far as these three woman could ascertain, if Tess kept up her work and took the classes they indicated, she would student teach as she originally planned. That would be after three semesters at Wind River.

What Tess had to do was dual enroll at both the cc and Wind River her next semester. As soon as they were offered she needed to begin her teaching certification courses at Wind River.

She told her aunt about that as soon as she learned what could happen for her.

"I'm so excited for you, Tess."

They held on to each other, jumping up and down, then hugging.

"Yeah, I'll be racing around all day long, from campus to campus. I'm sure glad they're near each other."

"I told you, and this is a promise, I'll be there for you and babe, for the first 8 weeks or so this summer. It's my pledge to you. Then we talked about you finding child care for fall semester."

"Actually Aunt Em I kinda already looked into that. Remember that I stay in touch with my two families I cared for during my earlier days in Farnon with mom. They've shared stories with me about how it works out to have a job and also to have to take a child to child care. And they told me what to look for in child care centers I'd be interested in, when that time comes next fall."

"Plus, my dear, nearly half our teachers have young children in various child care situations. I'll start checking in with them."

"Wow, that would be so great," she touched her aunt's arm from across the table where they were finishing dinner.

℘

"I can't believe it's taken me two weeks to get up the courage."

Craig blew out a breath as he looked down the table. The blue-eyed beauty had her head down on the table.

"I hope she's OK, maybe just resting."

He picked up his backpack and sat down in the chair next to hers.

"Miss, miss I'm just checking, are you OK?"

She lifted her head up in a slow fashion and turned to him.

"Gosh, thank you, I'm OK. I'm swacked out, just finished an exam that's about a fourth of my grade for this class."

"I'm Tess," she gave him her wide smile and looked into his dusky gray eyes.

She held out her hand and shook his.

"I'm Craig. I been sittin' at this table for weeks, and when I saw you with your head down, I decided I ought to check."

"This is my favorite study place; I get to look out at the beautiful trees, the sky, everything."

"Uh huh, and study some."

She began to laugh at his remark, then nodded to him as he joined in the laugh.

"Actually, I'm pretty sure I did well on the exam."

"Good for you, I gotta head out to class in a minute. You're studying?

"Teacher, elementary, course work here to transfer to Wind River after the summer, you?"

"Ag business, the AA, gonna take over the family farm."

"Wow."

He watched her eyes get big as she took in what that meant.

"Yeah, it's pretty much a half to."

She raised her eyebrows.

"A tale, for another day," he smiled and got up, grabbing his backpack.

"See ya, Craig."

"See ya, Tess."

℅

For the rest of that spring semester Craig sat at the same table where he and Tess studied.

They took one five-minute break from their studying, late each Monday through Thursday afternoon, after their last class. Tess spoke in very blunt terms about her situation. But so did Craig.

"I must let more love into my life," she spoke in quiet tones as she nodded her head to him.

He watched her nod. On these breaks they often stood next to the library windows, gazing out.

"Same thing for me, Tess, got pretty beat up in my last relationship, bottom line, she hated the idea of a life with someone, on a farm."

"You gotta appreciate her honesty, right?"

"That's true, and you certainly shared about the father of your child."

"That's right, I'm ashamed now." She shook her head and blew out a breath. "But it was a passion-filled time for me, and I sure did not love him."

"Sexual power over someone, it's a pretty strong emotion."

"Yeah, for sure, I am a manipulator," she paused, "you must think I'm a pretty terrible person."

His gray eyes penetrated her blue ones, and in a moment he spoke, "It's not my place to judge, just God's."

They returned to their studying.

The second week in April Craig shared with her at the end of a day, "Hey, I'll be out for three or maybe four days, Friday, classes Monday, Tuesday, and Wednesday. My teachers know. It's planting time, for sugar beets. I'm hopin' we'll be finished Tuesday. It'll be tough catching up after missing three days, but my teachers helped me move ahead. They really get it, two have Ag backgrounds."

"Don't know a thing about planting or about sugar beets, but good luck, you gotta get back, semester's over mid-May."

"Yeah, I know. You are beautiful, Tess. If you hadn't told me, I'd a never known you were going to have a baby."

"Carrying it inside, it's nice to be tall."

℘

"I'm glad you're joining us for Sunday dinner, Granddad."

Jack Palmerst tried to visit his daughter, Emily, and son, Joe, once or twice a year.

"It's April now, been since Thanksgiving that we've seen you."

"Right, and after we have the meal, I need to share with you two."

After they finished off the beef tacos, beans and rice they sat together in Emily's cozy living room.

"Coffee?"

"Please," Jack spoke up.

"I'll take some, want help?" Emily asked.

"I got this," Tess smiled to them.

Once they got settled, Jack handed Tess a sealed envelope. She saw a name on the envelope, an unfamiliar name. She noticed the flowing script of the handwriting.

Tess raised her eyebrows to her granddad.

"Uh huh, that is female writing, your grandma's."

He took a drink of the coffee from the mug and set it down.

"So, on your grandma's deathbed, our own bed in our bedroom, she shared with me about your dad, Tess. I've decided it's time to turn this situation over to you, 'cause it has to do with genetics, your family background."

"You mean about dad's appearance, a big blue-eyed blonde. And you, Emily, his sister," she paused and looked at Emily, "so dark haired and dark eyed, you and Granddad Jack, looking so much alike."

"Have you always wondered, Tess?"

"Uh huh, for a long time."

"Dad, what did mom say to you?"

"Well, Emily, she was very lucid for a little time; she wanted me to get a letter from her underwear and sock drawer. It was at the bottom of that drawer, and it was turned over so I almost missed it. I took it to her."

"Ethan Overridge," she spoke out the name on the envelope.

Granddad pointed to the envelope Tess held in her hands.

"I watched tears form in your grandma's eyes."

"Find this man," she pleaded, "he is Joe's biological father. Please don't tell Joe. Find the man and ask him to meet Joe."

Jack put his head down, holding it with his hands, his elbows on his knees. Tess saw his tears as he raised his eyes, looking first at Emily and then at Tess.

"Then grandma handed the envelope to me."

"Stay out of it, Jack," she whispered to me. "I've loved you both, you and Ethan. He's not far; he doesn't know, doesn't know."

Emily and Tess sat, numb, lost in their own thoughts.

Tess's mind whirled, "I always wondered about the brown eyes, the blue eyes, the much different look."

"Those words were the last she ever spoke to me. I'm turning this over to you, Tess. Find the father of your dad, 'cause it may help you determine some of your baby's genetics, at least on the Palmerst side of the family."

"Thank you, Granddad Jack. It could be a clue, about diabetes, heart conditions, epilepsy, different medical conditions, from this man's genetic background. And I can understand how upset you must have been to hear that news."

"As she was dying, shook me to my core."

Tess watched his dark eyes blaze with tears.

"I knew at that time I would not say anything to Joe, for a really long time in the future. I just knew I needed to love him. But now, a new generation of our family is beginning."

"So you're coming forward, with this. I'll do my best to search for dad's biological dad."

Emily spoke up, "And I can help. From working with my little ones, I know how important it is to have the family background."

"Bobby John's been great about that, sharing both his parents' medical situations. I know that's private information. And I've not yet had any physical issues, just the mess with my emotions."

She watched her granddad nod to her, "Which you seem to be handling, now."

"Yeah, a baby can do that to a person, force maturity; a vision for the future for child and mother."

"Thank you for the meal, and for helping me with this whole situation. I am so happy to be able to turn this over to you, Tess."

"I will research this name. One clue you gave me was that grandma said he is not far. Tell me again, how long for grandma?"

"She's been with God for over four years now."

&

Tess checked over her calendar; she had one week after her spring semester before summer school began. In eight weeks a whole semester's work occurred in summer school. She realized how hard she needed to work, and with a new baby.

"Hey, the babies I took care of, one three months old and one six months when I did summer babysitting, and there were three other kids in each family."

She thought back over those two summers.

"Aunt Em will help me," she told herself as she set back to work in the library. She pulled her mind to the task at hand; final exams loomed.

"I got this," became her standard answer to stressful times, because she visualized she would have a lot of them.

She and Craig continued their short conversations. They shared with each other about how much a person could learn about someone, in just five minutes time. He would graduate with his AA.

"Sheesh, I was one clueless guy when I started my classes. I've learned so much, a lot that I've shared with dad. And I am so glad my folks pretty much demanded I learn about the business of farming."

"How long you been at this?"

"Three and a half years, yeah you're lookin' at me and wondering why it took me so long."

"Spill."

"Fire, after one summer semester right out of high school, I quit the cc. I got the sugar beet crop in that October. Old wiring in the home I grew up in," he shook his head to Tess, "Mom and dad escaped, but the smoke inhalation, well, it changed their health big time."

"Scarred lungs?"

He nodded.

"After that?"

"House totally destroyed, all my stuff," he shook his head.

She saw the thin line of his mouth.

He went on, "They moved to town, Mom, totally finished with the farm scene. Dad told me if I helped him start over with the farmhouse, rebuild it from the basement foundation up, that it would be mine."

"Insurance on the place?"

"Uh huh, so he and I plus a bunch of subcontractors built it."

"Wow, a homebuilder."

"Yeah, among other things, hey, back to the books."

They returned to their studies until 5:15 that evening. The more time Tess spent with Craig the more interested she became in him. And she suspected that he wondered about her. He listened.

ℬ

"You got, maybe a week, before summer classes start, and baby, most any time, right Tess?"

She nodded to her aunt.

"Can I check this out with you? Talk to me."

"So, dad's biological father, by what your mom said, lives somewhere, maybe in southern Montana."

"Sweetie, this is a mighty big state, with a very long southern border."

"Right, so I've decided to pursue highway 95; there are towns along the way, west and east of Beet City."

Tess watched her aunt nod to her, smiling.

"Gonna take a road trip, a town a day, check in at the library, phone books, if they have a library; otherwise, at a city hall, place where employees might know a name, look in at the county seats of our two closest counties.

And that is the way Tess handled her week before summer classes started at the cc. Each day she drove home, further and further away from Beet City. And she kept telling herself not to get discouraged, that someday, one day she might locate her biological granddad.

Friday morning she got up early and headed out. She looked out her side window to see the rows and rows of wheat, and barley, and sugar beets, emerald green on the surface of the land with royal blue skies above. She did not see a cloud in sight. At about 11 a.m. she drove into the visitor parking lot of the county seat.

"This is it, Tess," she said out loud, "if I come up empty, I'll suspend my search, pray that my little one has no difficult genetics in its background. I know granddad will be disappointed. Maybe one day," she nodded and took her time getting out of her car. She could feel the baby weighing on the bottom of her insides.

She introduced herself to two different staff members at the courthouse. They sent her to a third area, the judicial division of the county. Tess spoke in quiet tones to this secretary after she introduced herself to Mona. It was the sincerity and politeness of this teen which prompted the secretary there to take Tess to an inner office.

"You spoke this name, Ethan Overridge, and that you are searching for him?"

"I am, a genetic background situation, it's all I can tell you."

"And you say you have a letter for this Ethan, from your grandmother, who handed the letter to your grandfather on her deathbed."

"She wanted the letter to get to this Ethan. And she said he was not far."

"This letter, important?" Mona nodded her head to Tess.

"Yes, to my dad and for me and the baby who is soon to be born."

"When for the baby?"

"Any time, I've been on the search for Ethan since Monday, just finished a semester of school. And Monday I start in again with classes at the community college in Beet City."

"You are one ambitious young lady."

Tess smiled, "I have big challenges ahead, raising a child, finishing school to become a teacher."

"Tess, Ethan Overridge is the judge for our county."

"Oh my," she paused as she gave the secretary a big-eyed look, "a lawyer?"

"Yes, he's filling in the rest of the term of a judge who recently died."

Her mind whirled as Tess thought of what news like hers might do to a man like this.

"What now?" Tess looked around the room, as she spoke out.

"Understand this," Mona nodded to her, "I can make sure Ethan gets this letter. We don't know what the letter says, but it's pretty obvious it's important information. Now, what Ethan does with the information, well, I can't say."

"And neither can I, but, Mona, I found out where he is and what he is. If that's all the further I get with my search, well, then I'll thank God that I have that much information. May I write a short note to go with the letter? And is it possible the letter and my note can go in a bigger envelope that's stamped personal and confidential?

"I can do that; write your note. You'll need to start back to Beet City soon. Leave me your name and phone number."

Dear Ethan,

Thanks to Mona for giving you this. My grandma, Donna Palmerst, gave this letter to my granddad, Jack, as she was on her deathbed. She asked him to please get this letter to you. The one thing she said to him was that 'you were not far.' Grandma's been gone four years now. Thank you.

Tess Palmerst

"I appreciate what you've done for me, also leaving my cell phone number for him," Tess said as she watched Mona put the note and envelope in the bigger envelope. She sealed the envelope and showed Tess the red personal and confidential stamp and Ethan's name on the outside of the envelope.

"This will be an inner-office mailing. Ethan will get this; I'll make sure of that."

"Thank you, Mona, and it's in God's hands as to what happens to the letter."

Tess rose from the table where she wrote the note, turned and shook hands with Mona.

"Tess, take care of your new babe, and keep up with the studying."

Tess nodded to her and left the office. Her tears came as she drove away from the county seat and headed back to Beet City.

"God's will, You been takin' care of me all this time, may I ask You to continue to help me."

She kept repeating that, her prayer, all the way back home.

∽

Beth Ann Palmerst arrived late on a Friday night, after Tess completed four weeks of summer school. Four weeks remained. On Monday morning Tess went to her classes.

When folks asked she simply replied, "I've just been through the most marvelous, most grueling event of my life. And I thank God for my healthy little girl."

Baby Beth had visitors. Tess did not see any of them, because she remained in class or studying all day, every day. Aunt Em stayed in charge of the baby. Visitors needed to come during the day. Night time Tess devoted to Beth, reading to her and preparing for bed. Every night, from the time Beth came home from the hospital, Tess sang songs to her. She sang little diddies as she bathed her baby girl, "Splish, splash, I was takin' a bath, long about a Saturday night," and "so big, so big," spreading Beth's arms out, and then taking her from the tub.

Grandparents, great granddad Jack, and Bobby John came to see Beth. Tess decided on bottle feeding, with her class schedule. So several folks had a chance to feed Beth and dote over her. And Tess wanted the baby awake as much as possible in the daytime, so she would sleep at night. Before bed and bottle songs included lots of Christmas tunes, starting with "Silent Night."

During the three weeks before her next term, Tess got final word of her admittance to Wind River College. She met her education academic advisor and also her Wind River transfer evaluator, the lady she worked with while she attended community college. That woman was key to Tess being able to transfer so much of her AP and community college coursework.

She carried Beth in her baby carrier as they visited the Wind River book store to pick up her books for classes Tess registered for this fall term. The books weighed heavily on her shoulders in her backpack, and with holding Beth's carrier she exclaimed, "Gosh, I got a real load, baby girl."

They made their way through the parking lot of the student center.

"Best news of all, Beth," she spoke to the baby as she secured her in the proper position in the sedan's back seat, "I have a good child care situation for you."

Her wide-eyed daughter waited for Tess to continue, "Yeah, I know you're starting to understand a lot of what I tell you. Anyway, you'll be with Miss Miriam, at the same child care center as a teacher at Aunt Em's school. What I mean is this teacher's daughter is with Miss Miriam also. That little girl is three months older than you, but you'll both be in the baby care unit. So I'll sorta know a parent, and you and Isabella will get acquainted.

The place you'll spend your days comes highly recommended. Your dad, Bobby John, has already paid for the first two months of your care there. He told me he would help me with child care and insurance for you, and so far, he's held up his end of the bargain."

Tess glanced back at her daughter as she headed for Aunt Em's.

"I love you, sweet Beth," Tess sang to her daughter, again and again as they headed home.

"One of these days you'll sing along with me," she looked back seeing Beth smile. From very early on after her birth, Tess got to say to folks, "Yeah, she's a smiler."

ℂ

"Tess, this is Craig Huntcrowe."

"Oh my gosh, how are you?"

"Sorry it's been so long since we've chatted, uh I need to say Happy Holidays. And I am fine. It was a long and difficult fall season. Do you have time to talk?"

Tess watched Beth sitting on the blanket on the living room floor. She played with rings and blocks.

"I do, hey you got the beets in."

"Right, and the barley, and, a little bit of soybeans; hardest thing though, my mom got sick."

"I'm sorry."

"The baby, your little one?"

"Beth Ann arrived Friday night half way through summer school. Super little baby, Aunt Em took care of her until her school started. Beth's with Miss Miriam, at a child care center."

"Not so many babies for Miss Miriam?"

"Five, Beth is youngest, they go up to 13 months, as soon as they're walking they move to another care taker. Back up, tell me about your mom."

"Lung problems, from the smoke inhalation at the fire that took my folks' farm home."

"Better now?"

"Yeah, but the damage, it's permanent. She's on oxygen some."

"My prayer is for each day to be special for her, as each day is special to you and me."

"Never more clear to me, Tess, God's in charge."

"So, I'm free for two weeks, now that my semester's ended at Wind River. I would like to invite you to lunch at Aunt Em's. It'll be before Beth's afternoon nap. And Aunt Em's still got a couple more days of school."

"That'd be great; I would like to see you again and meet your little one. She doesn't go to child care on your breaks?"

"No, her dad wants me to spend time with her when I'm not in classes. He pays for the child care, whether Beth goes or not."

They made plans and when Tess got off the phone she went to Beth. She plopped down next to her.

"Beth, I've invited a nice man to have lunch with you and me in a few days. I'm really feeling Christmas spirit. Some of that is the joy I have, you with me, my schoolwork moving on. Thank you for being such an easy baby to work with."

Tess watched a smile appear on Beth's face, and a slight nod of her head.

"Hey, I think you understand a bunch of what I say to you, already, making me flush with pride."

Tess nodded to her daughter and kissed her on her forehead.

℘

"Welcome!"

Tess looked from his smiling face to his hands.

"Wow, beautiful carnations, they smell spicy and wonderful."

"Thank you for inviting me to lunch; I'm starved."

"I figured you would be, soup, salad, sandwiches, chocolate chip bars, we'll get you filled up."

Tess hung his coat in the front closet. She turned with flowers in one hand and went to Beth.

Craig watched Tess kneel down and show Beth the red and white bursts of color.

"Beautiful!" she exclaimed to her daughter.

Craig stepped nearer to the mother and daughter.

He saw a smile appear on the baby's face.

Tess turned to Craig and handed the bouquet up to him.

"Please hold these; I'll pick Beth up and introduce her to you."

Tess made the introductions. Craig shook Beth's hand.

He looked from mother to daughter. Tess's black hair contrasted to the fine light hair Craig saw starting to grow all over Beth's head. And her greenish-blue eyes looked very different from the pale blue eyes of her mother. Tess had eyes, Craig noticed, that seemed always to be filled with light. He guessed that it was because of coloring of her corneas.

"Looking for resemblances?"

She watched him nod his head to her.

"So far, she's Beth, just looks like herself, they're some blue-eyed, but blonde genetics in the family background, a story for another day."

"Let's eat; you'll fix for yourself," Tess said as she led him to the kitchen.

"She's just now sitting in a high chair, likes it, and it's sure easier to feed her."

They ate together, Beth with her squash and peaches. Tess ate a ham and cheese sandwich and a small salad of spinach and carrots.

"A real trick, to eat, and to feed a little one. You definitely picked up the eating with one hand and feeding baby with the other."

Tess laughed, "Oh Craig, you've got such a gentle, sweet sense of humor."

They smiled to each other.

"What for dessert, you ask?"

"There's dessert, after all this?"

"Oh yeah, this crew has appetites."

They wanted to wait until Tess put Beth down for her afternoon nap. Craig followed her to the baby's room.

"Nice, this room's so warm and cheerful," he said as he watched her change Beth.

Craig stood and looked at the framed writing on the wall next to a window in Beth's room.

"Oh my, Tess, this piece on the wall, it's something you'll share with Beth one day."

"Mother Teresa, she's the model for me, of how to live my life. I already share what's in the writing," she paused, "with Beth, about being happy, honest, kind, giving your best. I find it positively amazing how well she listens, how much she seems to absorb about what I say. I talk to her about Mother Teresa; this nun's giving me a path to navigate my life."

"Are you Catholic?"

"No, I'm not, but I did a report on Mother Teresa in middle school. Her story had such an impression on me, 'cause I was going through chaos. She and my teachers, especially at Farnon High, well, they saved me."

They were quiet with each other for several moments.

"Kids in your life?" Tess asked.

"Older sister, in a neighboring town, three boys, what a blast they are."

"Get to see them much?"

"Nah, my sis sorta broke with the family over the farm."

"So it's yours now," she looked him in the eye, "with some money stipulations."

"Wow, and I never even talked about this with you when we took our breaks."

"A farm is a huge deal, but if she wasn't willing to do her share of the work," he paused, well," he shook his head to her.

"Right, we went through a lawyer, and I think kinda got things straightened out."

"Yeah, time will tell on these kinds of situations."

"Uh huh."

Tess leaned over and kissed Beth on the forehead.

"Sleep well, little one."

They watched Beth close her eyes.

Tess led Craig to the kitchen island. They sat next to each other after they got coffee and chocolate chip bars for themselves.

"How's this gonna work, your next few semesters?"

"Finished my first semester at Wind River this spring; summer, next fall, I'll student teach and graduate. Maybe I'll find a temporary fill-in position as a teacher in the spring after that."

"Doin' good?"

Tess gave him her wide smile, "Yeah, very good, I took classes at both the cc and Wind River in the fall. They thought I wouldn't be able to do it. But I did. Beth stayed healthy; I stayed healthy. It's all about time management, uh, like studying in 30 minute increments, positively amazing what a person can accomplish in 30 minutes."

"You have one heck of a lot of self-discipline."

"Yip, that's what it takes."

"And after you graduate, living here?"

"Nope, as soon as I get a job, Beth and I are moving away from Aunt Em. We gotta stand up on our own two feet. Tell me about your place, what your plans are for the next few years."

"Love, continue to search for that one person I want in my life, to share my life with me."

She turned and looked into his dusky gray eyes, "Someone who sees agriculture as a bright future in your world."

"Exactly, now you're reading my mind."

"Not, I remember early on you shared about a relationship that ended because she was not in the least bit interested in the farm life."

"Wow, I don't remember talking about that."

"Hey, but you did. And you shared about your love of the land, gonna be your land, and of feeding the world, as farmers do."

"Yeah, my sugar beets, and all the other farmers' beets, they'll help with the candy making."

"Never thought about that, yikes, what it'd be like if we didn't have sugar?"

"Stuff would taste sorta gross, in my estimation," he stuck out his tongue and made an ugly face for her to see.

"Agree," she smiled to him and shook her head.

"Tess," he turned to her, "I know you don't have time for a relationship now, and for the foreseeable future, but you need to know I want your friendship. And if it's OK I'd like to see you more often. And," he paused as he struggled with his words. He took a deep breath, "At some point I would want you to see my home, the land, explain about the farming, what my life is like, meet my family."

Tess gave him her wide smile, "I would like that very much, but I really couldn't do a special visit with you until next fall, my student teaching internship. And that would depend on where I'm sent to do my internship. And yes, at some point I would want you to meet my parents, also."

"With a child, will that make any difference?"

"I may have a chance to work, uh do the internship, in the Beet City area, to be close to Beth. So it may make a difference, a child," she nodded to him.

"Uh, your folks?"

"They live away from Beet City; I think I've told you, mom one direction, and dad and my stepmom, in another direction."

"Yeah, now I remember."

"How far outside Beet City is your family farm?"

"A couple of miles east, and on a paved county road."

"Hey, that's pretty sweet; you get plowed in the winter."

"I do, it's a matter of getting from the home to the road."

"Yeah, how do you handle that?"

"Trusty old pickup, I hook a snow scraper to the front of it."

"Goodness, you're all set up for Montana snow."

"I am, and I need to go. I'm getting involved in our local and state farm bureaus that work with the sugar beet operations and with lots of other crops. I'll share another time."

"Please, I know you do lots more than the farm operation."

She handed him his coat and watched him put it on.

"It's been fun to meet, to show you my world. Thank you for the flowers, Craig. Hey, I've not even acknowledged that you've graduated, that's wonderful."

They came into a hug. He kissed her, a gentle kiss, his lips caressing hers.

"Happy Holidays, Tess, to you and Beth."

She nodded as she opened the door for him. She stepped out after him and watched Craig turn and wave to her. She waved back.

"God bless and keep him. Once I get my student teaching under control, I want to get to know Craig better."

℘

Craig reviewed his visit with Tess. He spoke out as he drove away, "Just 17, with a child and a college education well under control. She's so lucky she has folks who believe in her, who're helping her with the finances. She's super smart, the lunch was delicious, and her aunt's home is in order. That's how she does it, organized, a place for everything. She loves her daughter, all kids, I think, and she's accepted the consequences of her actions, of just a short time ago, bringing a child into the world."

A little later he added, "And I wish for Tess," he paused, "I want the best for her, for her future. Please, God, help her."

3

"My fervent Christmas wish to learn more about this nice man, Craig, who he really is."

Tess prayed that many times a day. This Christmas week Tess stayed home with Beth, not singing with the Christmas Eve choir or helping with the Christmas Day meal at the Food Pantry. For the first time Beth ran a fever and slept in fits at night.

⁊◌

Granddad Jack pulled Tess aside as the two of them offered to do the clearing and clean up of the holiday meal. The family postponed the meal until Beth's antibiotic for her ear took hold.

"Any word, from Ethan?"

Tess looked into his dark eyes, "Been a few months, but I have hope. We don't know what happened in his world, through all these years. I just keep praying. And, honestly, Beth seems to be doing just fine. Her baby checks, with her pediatrician, all's well. Are you at all worried about dad, uh how Joe will take the news, if that ever happens?"

"Joe's got a solid head on his shoulders; he'll probably be angry some, but it's not on him, it's his mother."

Tess looked to him, hearing the bitter tone of her granddad's voice. They continued to work together at the dirty dishes. The rest of the family sat in Emily's living room, talking about this holiday season.

Marty checked in with Emily a week before the holiday dinner. It seemed to be working out OK that she brought her friend, Kyle. All the family kept their attention on Beth. Tess looked around, asking herself if a little child did mesmerize a family. Joe and Angela took Beth to her room for her afternoon nap.

"Hey, it appears that a baby can affect a whole family," Tess smiled to herself.

Her dad and Angela returned.

"She lay right down and is quiet."

"Yeah, at child care, the babies quiet down pretty fast. I kinda think they know that their families will be coming before long to pick them up. One thing little ones crave is consistency," Tess looked around to her family and nodded.

"Same thing in school, little children like to know what the plan is. I think it keeps them safe to know what comes next," Emily said.

"Sounds like a tip you'll be able to use with the children you'll work with, Tess."

"Right, and with Beth."

She watched the group nod their heads.

"Dessert, then I'll need to head out," Granddad Jack shared.

Tess liked Kyle, her mom's latest guy. He seemed friendly, managed an auto mechanic shop, and worked with his employees. She watched as her dad seemed to have the same pleasant reaction to the man Marty brought. And Tess thought, "Mom's trophy wife material, what is it with a guy who likes a beautiful woman on his arm?"

She remembered Bobby John, how he wanted to show Tess off when they went out.

"Yeah, it's a male ego trip," she thought as she returned to the conversations going around the room.

The group ate pie, pumpkin for some, and apple for others. They sipped the fragrant hazelnut coffee. Tess loved the taste and saved it for special occasions. Tess and Emily thanked family for visiting Beth as they left for their homes.

"I'm pleased, Aunt Em, with everyone's reaction to no toys or clothes for Beth. They seemed to appreciate that I've opened up a savings account in her name, and that I will put gifts of money in that account. This little girl will need all the help she can get as she gets older. On a teacher's salary, I'm afraid I won't be able to sock much away for her, uh, college, or for a home."

"Oh contraire," Emily smiled to her niece, "this home, I did it; I believed it was possible to become a homeowner."

"And you are, Aunt Em, and a lovely home it is."

Tess hugged her aunt as she heard Beth waking from her nap.

"Again, your hospitality, I could'a never done all I'm doing without you, and your help."

"And you two are a blessing to me, opening my eyes to family relationships, mother to daughter, so wonderful," she smiled and touched Tess's cheek.

ॐ

By mid-March, Tess felt assured she could finish, graduate after next fall semester and student teaching. But she had a scare, in February. Her teaching certification advisor called her in to let her know that a pre-requisite for her internship in the fall had not been fulfilled. Her advisor contacted the professor of the class Tess did not take. After visits with the professor, her advisor, and the chair of the elementary education program, it finally got decided that Tess could work out an independent study with the professor. She would be able to student teach in the fall, provided she met the prof's criteria for the study and did the work necessary.

Headaches and bouts of crying started for Tess as the end of April approached. She did everything the prof asked of her. And still that person would not let Tess know her grade.

"All I want to do is pass this independent study with a C or better."

She sought help from her advisor.

"He's a stinker, and a stickler; it's unfair, what's happened to you with this prof. We'll hope for the best. You must work hard on the rest of your classes. You've carried way too much of a load. But we understand what you want to do, an urgency to finish up."

They discussed the load of coursework Tess would take in the summer. It all seemed much easier than what she studied all through her last few semesters.

"And the best part, Mrs. Saylor, is that I get to take my two music classes."

"You talked very early about wanting to help with music in the schools."

"And I believe I will get to do that, maybe just help with music programs, like a Christmas program, wow" she nodded, "a dream I've had for a long time."

ℂ

Tess looked at her calendar, three days to the start of summer school. Her mom called her, just checking in.

"I just feel so numb; the last couple of weeks of the spring semester I only slept a couple of hours a night. That was just so totally stupid, to jam all of that into the semester."

"Sweet girl, you were warned. But you made it. And I am so proud of you." Tess heard the pleasant and heartfelt tone of her mom's voice.

They chatted about the schedule Tess would carry through the summer. She shared with her mom that Beth would go to child care most of the summer. Emily needed to take a class at Wind River, to help her with teacher recertification.

"It won't be long; you'll graduate, that'll be really something, Tess."

"Thanks Mom, my dream being realized."

A few minutes later she picked up the phone for a call.

"Tess, this is Ethan Overridge."

It took Tess a few seconds for the name to register.

"Uh, uh, oh Ethan, I wasn't sure I would ever hear from you."

"Well, you have."

Tears burst from her eyes, at his tone, and the shock of hearing his voice.

"I'm sorry," she spoke in a teary voice, "it's that."

And then she stopped.

"I would like to meet with you; what about this Saturday afternoon?"

"Yes, I could ask my aunt to watch my little one for a couple of hours."

They agreed on a location and time, at a busy truck stop restaurant outside Beet City. She gave him a description of herself. Tess told her Aunt Em and asked for help watching Beth.

And just like that, after nearly a year of Tess praying and hoping they met.

She looked for a man waving as she entered the truck stop café and looked around.

"Ethan," she shook his hand after he stood at the table.

"Tess."

They sat next to each other at a small table in a corner of the big café. She heard the noise level of many voices around her.

Tears trickled down her cheeks as she shook her head, looking into his blue eyes. She held her hand to her throat; it hurt from seeing him.

"Dad, dad looks so much like you."

"Oh yeah, me, an older version?"

She nodded as she saw a smile on his face and a more pleasant tone to his voice.

"What happened, Ethan?"

"My minister told me it was time to see you, to meet my granddaughter."

She gave him a wide-eyed look, shaking her head, "Uh," she stopped, "you, my biological grandfather."

"That's right; what's your dad's name?"

"Joe, Joseph John Palmerst, he's 34, my folks were 17 when I was born."

"And your granddad?"

"Jack Palmerst."

"So, your grandma, Donna, and I met at the sheriff's department in the county where your grandparents lived."

"I remember; she did administrative work there."

"And I was a newbee lawyer, working in that county and two others."

"You two became interested in each another."

"Uh huh, even though we were both married."

"It happened."

"It did, the holiday season of 1966. Two months, I'll love your grandma even beyond death, she's here."

He patted his heart. Tess watched his shoulders jerk forward and his head go down. She heard his tear-choked voice.

"But she never contacted me about your dad during all those years. She did pretty much say it all in the letter you delivered to me. It was her wish. And I am so grateful that your granddad, despite his probable anger, and sadness, followed through with what she wanted to do."

Tess took photos from her jacket pocket.

"Dad, born late August, 1967," she showed Ethan the color picture of her dad taken last Christmas.

"Oh, dear God," Ethan whispered as he turned away from Tess.

He choked as the tears again came to his eyes. Tess touched his upper arm to comfort him.

"There is no doubt; he really is a younger me."

Tess put down another picture, of her grandparents, her granddad with his coal black hair and dark eyes, and her grandma, with blonde hair, that year.

"Donna, oh Donna," he whispered as he touched the picture, the part with her grandma.

The third picture she laid on the table was of Tess and Beth.

"Oh my goodness, a great granddaughter."

He took a moment to look closer at the picture.

"You both are so beautiful," he looked into her pale blue eyes.

"Thank you."

"Here's what's happened, uh, after the initial shock of the letter. I sought counseling. I may be a judge now, but I sure as heck don't have all the answers. And as I mentioned to you it was my minister who strongly suggested I should meet you and go from there."

"Refill on your coffee?" Tess asked.

"Please, I drank that cup down so fast, wanting to drink something before I launched in."

Tess got the waitress's attention.

After their refills, he began again.

"My wife, terribly upset, when I told her. Then she remembered how rocky our marriage was during the fall of 1966. Your grandma, Donna, and I talked a little bit about leaving our marriages. Uh, say again when Joe was born?"

"Late August, 1967."

"Dear Lord," Ethan covered his face with his hands and shook his head back and forth.

Tess watched tears squeeze from his eyes when he took his hands away.

"Our son, David Andrew, was born in late August, 1967, our only child."

"Two sons, two different women, oh Ethan."

He took out his wallet and showed Tess a picture of the three of them, taken at David's law school graduation.

"Your wife?"

"Holly."

"Ethan, Holly, and David Overridge, where is he, uh, practicing?"

"Alabama, with the State Attorney's office, he's married, did so late. My grandson, Josh, he's 6."

They paused for a moment, "So much I want to ask you."

"Joe had you early, right?"

"Yeah, he was 17 when I was born, and my daughter, Beth, was born when I was almost 17."

"And your dad, Joe, my son, share about him. I can't imagine how he will react to all this news."

"Dad had a good early life with Jack and Donna. Two years after he was born Emily came along. Joe and my mom, Marty, were high school sweethearts, married before graduating, and I came along immediately. Almost as quick, they divorced, my mom drinking way too much, not taking care of me. So Joe was a single parent, raising me the best he could. He managed, still does, the city government facilities division in the small community down the road, Banton.

He remarried when I was 11. I hated my stepmother and made life hell for my dad and her. So ashamed of this," Evan watched her face flare red, "it got so bad my dad had to ship me to my mom, for better or worse. I was destructive to his second marriage."

"What caused your actions, so terrible?"

"I loved him, way too much, emotionally destroying me. I should'a gone to counseling. But dad decided on the direct approach."

"And living with your mom?"

"Bad, pitiful, the first couple of years, I finally realized I had to straighten out or end up in jail. She basically did not care, but I think she was trying to pull herself together, as I started to get better. The schools helped us, both, so much. My teachers saw my promise, that's what saved me. I'm really smart, and I started to love school, love learning. Hey, this is about you, the rest of my story is that Beth came into my world, and college became a goal I could reach, so far, so good."

"You are a bright, fine spirit in this difficult world, Tess."

"Thank you."

"What now, Tess?"

"Don't know, you're a lawyer, and a judge, I feel pretty certain you've dealt with situations kinda like this."

"Right, but not personal, this whole situation makes my heart hurt, father-feelings for a son I never knew about. But I'm the kind of person who takes responsibility for my actions."

"As I did when I found out about having a baby. As I've always believed, a child is a gift from God," she nodded her head and smiled to Ethan.

"Yes, I believe that."

"So, maybe meet Joe's dad, Jack, and Joe, at the same time, or Joe alone."

"That's sounds pretty much like how we need to handle it, that's all depending, on your family."

"I'll make the next moves, Ethan; I have just a little time before my all-important summer school starts. I'll contact Granddad Jack, find out how he would like to handle the next step, getting you and Joe together. He's been super understanding through all this. Donna and you, a situation he did not know anything about, until she lay dying.

Hey, the reason I got involved in this was my baby's genetics; were there bad genes in the background of the family, mental illness, diabetes, epilepsy? What we bring to our children, it's scary, our backgrounds."

"I agree, you're very young to see the dangers in family genetics."

"Yeah, I tune in real close to kids, to what's going on with them, in my babysitting, with Beth now, with all the students I've been in contact with, and then student teaching ahead."

"Have you seen stuff?"

"Uh huh, epilepsy, a grand mal, in the classroom I was observing in, and another situation, diabetic shock; unbelievable what sips of juice can do for a diabetic little one."

"As far as I know, we don't have difficult stuff in my background, hopefully Joe doesn't have problems."

"Nope, he's in good health, so is my mom; it's just that Grandma's cancer, a shock, cancer's just a different beast."

"Right," he paused and nodded to her, "here's a picture of me at Joe's age, and I'm giving you a copy of the letter Donna wrote to me. I would want Joe to see it. Thank you for meeting with me. I feel about a thousand percent better after our conversation."

Tess smiled to him, "I'm sure you had a vision or two about me, after seeing a lot of teenagers in your courtroom situation."

They stood away from the table.

"May I hug you," he paused and she saw his smile, "granddaughter?"

"Of course."

They said their goodbyes. Tess left to return home to her daughter and Ethan stayed at the table, making phone contact with his family.

℘

Tess called Granddad Jack several hours after she arrived home from her visit with Ethan.

"Thank you, Tess, for doing this. From what you've explained he's a reasonable man, a judge, a responsible father."

"Granddad, Ethan spoke of his love for Grandma Donna, that it would be for all time. Do you think it's possible for a man to love two different women, so deeply?"

Tess heard silence.

"Sweet girl, oh yes, I think it is very possible."

"Your plan?"

"Yes, after all this legwork you've done, I will meet with Joe, alone, in a week or pretty soon. Is it possible, well of course you asked, did Ethan happen to give you a picture of himself?"

"He did and a copy of Donna's letter. I'll mail those to you so you can have them when you meet with Joe. I decided it was none of my business what the letter from grandma said. I have not, nor will I ever read it, but Ethan's picture, oh wow."

"Yeah?"

"Yeah, Granddad."

℘

"We haven't talked about your spring semester."

"Nope, you go first, Craig. I'm so glad you called, a date, out to dinner."

He watched her beaming smile.

"Got the crops in, the beets, barley, soybeans, and a small field of drought-resistant wheat."

"Good, and your home, family?"

"Home's fixed up the way I want it; always will be work to do, the yards, front and back, this summer. I planted trees a couple years ago and they are taking off."

"Family," she paused, "wanta order first?"

She watched him nod.

Her mind whirled, "Maybe only the second real date I'd ever been on, actual out to dinner, so nice."

Tess decided on what she wanted to eat. She sat in silence after they ordered.

"You're quiet."

"Uh huh," she looked into his dusky gray eyes, a shock of black hair combed into place.

"Mom's dying; her lungs're so ravaged."

Tess touched his upper arm.

"I am so sorry; how can I help?"

"Prayers, for the morphine to continue to make her comfortable."

"It'll be pneumonia?"

He nodded to her.

"Soon?"

He brushed away a tear.

"And after she's gone to God?"

"More prayers, mainly for dad, he's spending a bit more time on the farm. I think now that the farm, being outside on the land, working, it soothes him. He'll find his way, very tough man."

"And what about you?"

"I'll grieve, but it will be a relief, especially for mom."

"Uh, is it too soon to meet your family?"

"Right," he nodded to her. "A picture of mom's the best way for me to show her to you. She's unrecognizable now."

Their food arrived, and they ate hearty. Tess looked around the friendly restaurant, always comparing wherever she ate with the food and atmosphere of the café where she worked in Farnon.

"Uh, I waitressed in a little café on Main Street in Farnon, slave wages, fall of my senior year. So I always check a place out."

"And?"

"Nice, a friendly and warm restaurant; this is really nice, Craig, and the food is tasty."

"And you're sweet company, believe me it is so good to see you."

"It's gotta be tough, when you see a lot of sickness."

"For sure."

"So, spring semester, difficult, many hours, still want to be a teacher. One thing I've learned," she shook her head in silence.

"This ain't no eight hour a day job, the one you'll take on."

"Absolutely, I'm always thinking about that, always will be planning at night, weekends; it'll always be with me, 'til the semester is done. Then we're on to the next semester."

"It's the circle of life," he gazed into her eyes.

"Wow, you're really tuned in," she gave him a wide-eyed look.

They talked a little about Beth and her antics.

"She's a great kid," Tess nodded.

They decided to walk around the neighborhood near the café before going home for Tess.

"It's not the right time or place to talk about my dad, save it, Tess," she told herself as he walked her up to Aunt Em's porch.

They hugged at the door. This night Craig kissed her forehead.

"Good luck with your summer school. I hope you get the internship placement you want."

"Take care, Craig, and thank you for a lovely evening."

After she got inside, she felt it again, a deep sexual ache for this very nice man.

Craig felt an arousal he had not had for a very long time.

ℰↃ

Fall 2003

"You must be thankful for the student internship assigned you, Tess, don't be a dope," she kept telling herself after she met for the first time with the mentor teacher at Bellwood Elementary.

Mrs. Baltimer worked with third and fourth graders for nearly 15 years at that school. She asked Tess about her past couple of semesters. After Tess summarized the coursework, Mrs. Baltimer smiled and nodded to her.

"Goodness, you fast tracked through all of this, and your little girl?"

"Right, Beth is two, walking, talking, singing, which we've always done together. It's unbelievable the pictures and words she totally understands from the storybooks we all read to her. I live with my Aunt Emily. She's my hero; gave me a home to live in, and helped me with tuition. She's a teacher, so supportive of me all through my life."

"She's elementary?"

"Yes, Emily's always worked with little ones, mostly third through fifth grade."

"I found your application especially interesting because you want to work with music programs, in addition to your elementary assignment."

"Yes, and when I saw what the various projects you're assigned to, in the fall, including the Christmas presentation, well it's why I hoped you'd pick me."

Tess smiled to her mentor.

"My dear, I believe we will get along just fine."

For the rest of that first meeting they discussed the third grade assignment. Tess left the school with a big smile plastered on her face.

"My goal, I'm starting to reach it."

She raised up her hand as she spoke and gazed up toward the sun. She observed the older red brick single level building, her placement until the end of the semester.

"It felt warm, homey, in Mrs. Baltimer's classroom."
Tess skipped along to her car.
"I am so happy," she spoke out as she got in.

℘

For two weeks Tess assisted in class and observed the students, helping out almost from the minute she joined the students her first day. Mrs. Baltimer stepped back and let Tess take over. By the end of September Tess felt a comfort level with her students that she could hardly believe. She understood them and already had parent conferences with three parents. She felt concern for the students. Classroom behavior improved for two of them.

Tess sat in a staffing for the third student. It involved the school principal, her mentor, Mrs. Baltimer, the school counselor, the school nurse, and the single father.

When it was over, Tess returned to her classroom. The students got back from a once a week art session.

"I was like that kid, out of control, with my mouth, maybe medication would'a helped me. But I think the little guy is just mad as hell at his circumstances."

That's what she decided.

By the first of November she saw an improvement in the boy. Every day she just told him to keep trying. She had a chance to talk to him about her own circumstances.

"I just kept trying, Trevor, please, you keep trying."

"I will, Miss Palmerst."

℘

Late Sunday morning of that first week in November she got a call from her mentor.

"Tess, I've talked to the principal and he agrees with my recommendation. I'm headed for emergency gall bladder surgery in a little while. I've been having pain, but, well you know."

"Right, the students come first."

"But my surgeon says I come first."

"Exactly."

"I just got started on the Christmas program planning, no theme. It'll be up to you to carry it through."

"I absolutely can do that."

"I've had a co-leader on this project in past years. But that teacher has left and her replacement does not want to help out, since it's her first year at Bellwood."

"Got it. God bless and keep you through your surgery and recovery."

"Thank you, Tess, you've been in charge for some time now. I'm so blessed to have you."

℘

"This'll be easier than I thought, a program," Tess spoke out after she got off the phone with her mentor.

"Oh Tess, don't be too sure about that, the ease of a program," she shook her head, reexamining what she just said.

During that fall semester at Bellwood the faculty worked with students on the themes of kindness to others and giving back. And Tess found the proper song to implement those themes. It came to her as she began singing Christmas songs to Beth in early October. Beth picked up on some of the melodies and knew a few words to the songs. So the King Wenceslas song Tess sang to Beth, it was her decision for the program.

Tess wrote out the narrator parts, the actions for King Wenceslas and his page in the great hall as they planned on rescuing the cold man. They found the poor man gathering fuel, and brought him back inside the castle where they got him warm and fed him. Students would act as servers to bring the poor man food and drink. While they were out in the winds and bitter weather, the monarch asked his page to follow in his footsteps to stay warmer.

Students from each of the five grades would sing part of a stanza of the song and the narrator would finish with the particular chorus humming the melody of the words to the stanza.   At the end of the fifth stanza the singers grew silent and the narrator spoke out, "Ye, who now will bless the poor, shall yourselves find blessing."

She planned that the fifth grader who played the song on the piano at the back of the stage would step forward with all the singers, five from each of the five grades, and the actors: king, page, the poor man, and the food helpers. Once they bowed the narrator asked the audience to join in with "We Wish You a Merry Christmas."

Tess got her holiday show approved by the principal.

"Miss Palmerst, I appreciate you following on with a Christmas program that suggests this year's school themes, kindness and giving back."

He handed her the paperwork she prepared for him.

"Both the story and the music interact well. How did you decide on this song?"

Tess nodded to Mr. Ingram and laughed.

"Hey, I started singing holiday carols to my little one in October. For whatever reason she liked the music and words to the story; that it told of a king who cared for a poor man."

Her next project was to find a time when she could practice with each group of singers. And she knew that the fifth graders would anchor the program. They would need strong voices. She went to the teachers of these 10 classes, 2 classes for each of the five grades. The teachers gave her the names of students with strong speaking voices and who seemed to be able to carry a tune.

Each night she talked to Aunt Em and Beth about her holiday project.

"I'm so glad to see you excited about your holiday program, Tess. You can imagine, once you get to your own school as a faculty member, how much fun you'll be able to have."

Tess spent several late afternoons setting up the sound system on the stage, with good-sized speakers to project voices. The microphones picked up sounds well. Another student teacher worked with her, listening for sounds toward the back of the school gym.

As the program came together, she and the designated students worked in the music room.

Tess felt sad about music at her school. Three different elementary schools shared the one music teacher. She realized the small amount of work that teacher could accomplish while being with students for such a short time.

℘

"I am so glad we can use the music room. And I am so glad you all can read music."

The program group agreed that it was the one thing they eventually learned from their short time in music class, reading music. They sang the melody, learning their lines. Voice projection was a goal Tess emphasized. They all began to understand that with this story of the king, well, if the audience could not hear clearly, the message would fail. The message was to be kind and to give back.

With the fifth graders' help, a one-page program got developed, so that the audience knew the story enacted on the stage, knew who the characters were, and the message got repeated three times somewhere within the singing. And, most important, Tess emphasized that the whole sound system might fail, that the students must project their voices. She shared a case of that happening to her during her elementary grades. In several instances Tess went back to the classrooms to ask for students with louder voices. She did get students with improved speaking and singing voices.

"Wow, this kinda stuff takes up so much time, coordinating my time with the singers plus my time working with my third graders," she murmured.

"But you want to do a good job, so it's worth it," several teachers mentioned to her after she talked about the time element.

Tess saw their smiles. She believed them.

The students decided to call the program *The Good King*. The difficult name of the king, Wenceslas, would be spoken only at the beginning of the singing of the first stanza. Tess checked her mailbox in the teacher workroom at the end of the day, that first Friday in December.

The message asked her to call her mentor at home. Tess checked around her colorful classroom, with holiday decorations in place, but not too many. She kept an orderly and organized classroom. Then she sat down and called.

"Mrs. Baltimer, I was surprised to hear a young man's voice."

"Oh yes, our son's home from school. He's finished his semester very early but starts again in early January."

"Guess I've forgotten you've got a youngster in college."

"For sure, we do indeed."

"I'm pleased at how well things are going, in the classroom and with the holiday program."

"I wanted you to be aware, I won't be returning to the classroom until next semester. There have been complications and other discoveries as a result of the surgery, the gall bladder situation. I will need for you to finish off your work at school, through that second week in December. Then I know you graduate. But I will ask you to double check the plan lessons for that last week, uh, for the sub, before semester break. We'll talk about grades, when you get to near the end of your time at school. You've kept me updated on how students are doing. But you really are their teacher, actually have been since a few days after you arrived."

"That sounds like a plan."

"God's been in charge, and He for sure gave me the best possible situation for my students, to have you there, guiding them. And I understand the holiday program is moving along."

"It is; I'm having so much fun. I explained to our principal that I needed a small contingent of each of the five grades to accomplish what I wanted to do, tell the story of the kind king. He agreed that I should not take on a big production."

"One day, of course you'll welcome that."

"Take care, Mrs. Baltimer, we will carry on. You must get to feeling better."

"Right, my gastroenterologist assures me that I will be ready to return to my students in January. God bless and keep you and all our students."

Tess heard her mentor's emphasis on *our*.

After she hung up, Tess went right away to the lesson plan book to take a look over what remained of her assignment, without her mentor.

"Me, telling a substitute what to do. Oh my, Tess Palmerst, you have come a long way," her mind whirled over the past years since she graduated high school.

Tess and Emily decided to wait for Christmas planning until Tess finished her semester. That way Tess could devote much time to the holiday program. She decided she needed to be on stage to guide the singers and keep the accompanist on track.

"We have a big job to do, represent our whole school. We can do this, correct?"

"Yes we can, oh yes we can," the group shouted as they started practicing in the gym on the stage. They all did a quick happy dance and then settled down.

"We only get to do this three more times, that's practice on the stage," she waved her hands to the group.

"Miss Palmerst, we are so glad you will be up here with us, even though it's just us who'll see you."

"Right," she paused and looked from one face to the next, until she saw each performer, "and are you glad a piano is here?"

"Yes," they all shouted out.

"What about Brianne, our piano player, who keeps us in control?"

"Awesome," one student spoke out.

Tess smiled as she heard claps, cheers, and whistling.

§Ω

With one week to go for her, and the performance on a Thursday afternoon, at 1:30 p.m., Tess felt numb as she walked out of school late Monday afternoon.

"Pick up Beth, check on the graduation schedule, get ready to turn in my end-of-internship paperwork," she spoke out as she wiped tears away. She drove into the parking lot of the child care center.

"You can do this, Tess, remember the semester at both Wind River, and the cc, oh yeah, you can do this."

Still, she had to wipe away the tears before she walked in. She did not want Beth to see her cry. Tess took in a deep breath and put a big smile on her face.

"I'm so glad to see you, Beth. Mommy's been crazy busy."

"King pogram?" Beth asked.

"Right, almost through it, performance soon."

"Then Mommy happy?"

"Yeah, less stressed," she told her daughter as she put her in her car seat for the drive to Aunt Em's.

"Let's sing, Mommy."

And so they began the first of three Christmas songs, "Silent Night."

"She's got a melodic voice," Tess whispered as they got ready to sing the second song, "Jingle Bells."

℘

"I know it's crazy times for you, but could we talk for a minute?"

"Goodness, Craig, it's so good to hear your voice."

"Yeah, I just got back from a farm convention in Iowa. When does your school group perform?"

"Thursday, 1:30 p.m., the next day's my last, gotta get back, finish up my internship paperwork and complete that class at Wind River. Then, my goal, I'll graduate."

"Wow, your world's gonna change, big time."

"Too much, too fast, my mind just swirls some of both my sleeping and awake hours."

"You've had tougher semesters."

"Yeah, I have, not so much studying as just finishing up everything. I'll spend part of a period explaining the final week to a substitute hired to finish the semester for Mrs.

Baltimer. Can you imagine, me, a student teacher, explaining to a credentialed person what to do?"

"Uh huh, I can, you're a take charge person, Tess. We'll talk again. Good luck with your program."

"Thanks, my students, they got this."

"I hear the tone of your voice, it's a tone of confidence."

ଛ

She couldn't help it. She felt tears burn her eyes as she watched her program students move to the front of the stage. The narrator lined up, with the page, the poor man, the king, and the servers. They bowed. They moved to the back, behind the simple props. The singers, all 25 of them, lined up and bowed. The accompanist stood by herself and bowed after the singers stepped back. Two fifth graders came toTess, each took a hand and led her to the center of the stage. The whole stage bowed along with Tess.

She heard clapping and whistling.

"I can't stop my tears, kinda overwhelmed," she nodded her head as she whispered.

She squeezed the hands of the students who held hers. The performance seemed to her to have taken just a few seconds. In truth, 14 minutes was the time element.

"I'm so glad the students helped me create a story page for our audience. Otherwise, it would'a been a hard story and song to understand."

Her cleanup crew went to work, removing the table and chairs, including a plate of bread and cheese, and a cup of liquid where the king, page, and man sat. Once she finished helping she sent the students back to class and took several minutes to disconnect the sound system.

She put her bag of notes and gear over her shoulder and bounded down the steps to the gym floor.

"Oh happy, how it turned out," she whispered as she strode along the side of the gym floor.

She looked ahead, to the back of the gym near the doors. A tall, dark-haired man smiled to her. She watched his smile get wider.   She stopped abruptly, her memory swirling.   He walked toward her and opened his arms to her.

Tess felt frozen in place as he came to hug her.

"Your students, they did a very nice job."

"Oh Craig, you saw it, our performance."

She stepped away from him, "Could you hear what they sang, the chorus, speakers, what they said?"

"I could."

"Wow, I'm so glad, needed another adult's opinion, someone not seeing the performance before."

"The notecard with the explanation, that helped."

"I'm pleased, then," and for the first time she smiled to him.

"I, I just," she paused, "shocked to see you here."

"Wouldn't have missed it, been on my calendar since you first mentioned it to me."

"You're interested in what I do," she nodded to him.

"You'll be a great guide for young people, Tess."

She felt his warm hand as she held it in both of hers.

"Gotta get back, my kids'll be getting antsy.   Another student teacher watched over them for me for a little while before, and now, after."

"Take care."

"Oh my gosh, thank you for coming, Craig."

"I'll call you, I know you got school, graduation, and Christmas coming up."

"Yeah, thanks for understanding."

Her throat started to ache as she thought of him, caring enough to see this little performance. She held her hand to her throat as tears squeezed from her eyes. She stood in front of her closed classroom door. Tess took in a big breath and walked in.

She watched as her class stood and clapped for her. Now she felt tears streaming down her cheeks. She mustered a little smile and nodded to all of them. Miss Gillam came to her and hugged her.

"It turned out wonderful, just the right length, especially for the little ones."

"Thank you, and I appreciate you watching my class."

"Yeah, they did great, both here and in the gym. And I liked the semi-circle setup of all the chairs for the students, like in a real theater."

Tess and her students agreed that they should read the novel they were working on in class. She let students read, then she read. The school day ended, and Tess walked out into the cold Montana sunlight.

"Thank you, God, for watching over me, and all of us."

℘

"Leaving my students, that was so super hard for me," Tess smiled to her internship coordinator.

"You had a good experience?"

"Oh yes, you and Mrs. Baltimer felt I could handle the class and the holiday program."

"We knew you could; I've looked through your paperwork that you finished up regarding your internship. I'm very pleased."

"I hoped that would be the case; I'm ready for my own classroom. I've turned in all my paperwork for both substitute and teacher credentialing for the state of Montana."

"You'll do subbing if you can't find something?"

"Right, midyear is very hard to find a position, except a real emergency."

"Those happen, your mentor, Mrs. Baltimer, she might have had a situation like that."

"I'm glad she did not, 'cause it's so hard on little kids if they see a lot of different subs. Thank goodness, she got sick, when I could help out."

The coordinator smiled to her, "Her students got really lucky, to have you there."

"That's what I believe."

Tess stood up from the table as her coordinator did. Tess shook hands with Mrs. Larez.

"You graduate, also?"

"I do, next week."

"Congratulations and best of luck in your job search."

"Thank you, I check opening positions often."

She walked with her head up and a smile on her lips after she left the coordinator's office. Tess stopped and moved to the side of the walkway, filled with students heading for their classes at Wind River. The cold blast of December wind took her breath away. She gasped for air.

"One more step along my way to my future," she whispered and started to cry. She found her car in the student parking lot and headed to Aunt Em's.

"Get a tree, please Tess," her aunt asked her that morning

She stopped at the Christmas tree lot, still with tears in her eyes.

"Next year, Beth, you'll come with me. I must be crying tears of relief, maybe disbelief," she shook her head as she spoke out. "Here you are, perfect little tree, a blue spruce, 4 ½ feet tall."

It fit great in her big trunk. She took it to Aunt Em's and set about decorating the spruce. Once she tried the lights and knew that they worked she put on a few ornaments. It was time to pick up Beth so she returned to the child care center.

"Mommy, mommy, carr me, hol me, miss you."

"And I miss you."

Tess put Beth's bag over one shoulder and picked her up, adjusting the little girl on her other hip.

℀

"You've done it, you have," her dad hugged her as they stood together in the back of the college gym. She moved to her mom.

"Honey, I am so proud of you," Marty whispered to Tess as they hugged. Granddad Jack and Aunt Emily came into a three way hug with her.

Tess turned in her gown at the return station outside the gym. Her aunt gave her specific instructions, "Meet at home, right away, OK?"

She drove her car to Aunt Em's and saw several different cars parked up and down the street. One of them she did not recognize.

"Congratulations," she heard her family shouting and clapping as she walked into the home she shared with Aunt Em these past few years. She felt tears spurt from her eyes.

"I'm so shocked to see you; I thought the plan was to all meet at a restaurant after stopping here."

Aunt Em stepped next to her and held her shoulder, "Nah, that was to get you to come home so we could each spend a few moments to honor you. I'll pick up Beth at the usual time. This is a celebration of you."

Tess took her bag to her room and tried unsuccessfully to take in deep breaths to calm herself. When she returned, Marty handed her a glass of sparkling cider. The family raised their glasses. Joe gave a congratulatory toast to honor her. They all sipped the cider.

He stepped from the back of the group to stand beside Granddad Jack. Tess did not notice him in the flurry of coming home. She stepped forward toward her dad.

"Dad," she spoke to him and then she looked behind him and to the left.

Ethan Overridge stood, smiling to her. Tess felt the constriction of her throat, unable to swallow. Tears welled up in her eyes.

"Oh my," she croaked out.

Ethan moved toward her, "Congratulations, dear Tess."

They hugged. Tess stood back away from him.

"Who, who?"

"Me, daughter," Joe paused, "I invited him."

"Thank you, Dad. I've sure missed out on what's happened to my own family's world."

Tess moved to the dining room table seeing the cake with white frosting, and red and green signage, "Congratulations, Tess."

Emily cut cake for all of them and they joined Tess in the living room. She sat on an ottoman with her family gathered together. They ate cake, delicious carrot, and drank the sparkling cider.

"Dad, Granddad Jack, Ethan," she stopped, shaking her head.

"I'll start," Joe said.

"It's taken a while," Granddad Jack nodded to the group.

"Dad came to me, with the letter from grandma and the picture of Ethan. I sure thought I was lookin' at myself when I first got a look at the picture. Genetics, in our case, truly told the story."

"I really took my time, going back in my memory to that holiday season in 1966, when Donna and I struggled so hard. But we did reconcile," Granddad Jack nodded.

"And Holly and I, we also continued in our marriage. But, as I told our granddaughter and I'll tell what I still know, "I love Donna, even beyond death.""

Tess nodded to Ethan, "He told me that, when we first met those years ago, before Beth, actually the week that Beth would be born."

Aunt Emily stood, "And God continues to bless us mightily, during this beautiful season, of Christmas and the graduation of Tess."

"Donna," Jack stood and gazed around at his family, "we hope you will have Christmas in heaven, as we'll enjoy it here on earth."

"Hear, hear," Joe spoke out, "Mom, one day we'll join you."

Tess watched Ethan nod his head. She felt that hope. Her own tears began to pool in her eyes.

৪৩

"Bellwood Elementary, you've been good to me," Tess spoke out as she gathered her folders together. She finished her meeting with the principal. The night before she went to Mrs. Baltimer's home. They decided on grades for her students. The semester would be completed in just a few days. The principal seemed satisfied with the way the semester turned out, with the students getting the help they needed.

Tess walked out of the school where she worked with the students to the best of her ability that fall semester. She said her goodbyes to the students the day before. The substitute would finish up next Tuesday, the last day for students and staff before holiday break. She turned around and looked back at Bellwood Elementary. She smiled and nodded her head, then headed for her car.

"I have one more task, tomorrow. I'm excited."

4

Christmas 2003

"Thank you for seeing me on such short notice, Miss Palmerst."

"I'm happy to talk with you. As I mentioned on the phone I've completed with my internship, graduated, my paperwork is turned in at teacher credentialing with the state of Montana. I am ready to take on a teaching assignment."

During the week after she graduated she got a phone call from a small elementary school on the outskirts of Beet City. A school administrator contacted teacher placement at the college. Tess's name appeared on the list of prospective teachers wanting positions midyear.

"It's such a busy time for all folks, this holiday season. And you've completed your work; your mentor at Bellwood and your internship coordinator are very pleased with your abilities with students. May I ask, how old are you and I know you don't have to answer."

She nodded to him, "It's OK, I get asked that a lot; I'm 19; I went year round, graduated high school early."

"My gracious, you show discipline, and perseverance, that's for sure, to do all this, maturity and initiative."

"Right, I have a 2 ½ year old daughter, my reason for being. And I am looking for a teaching position," Tess smiled to Mr. Jameson.

"Our situation is this; we lost Mrs. Carpenter after Halloween. A driver ignoring a red light t-boned her. She died at the scene. Her group of fourth graders, devastated, substitutes and school personnel tried to cover for this wonderful teacher."

He stopped talking and shook his head, attempting to get a handle on his emotions, "I'm sorry, it's, it's."

"Let me give you a minute, Mr. Jameson."

"Thank you, Miss Palmerst."

With a wobbly voice he started again after a short time, "But it's gone poorly. We would like you to try the position for two weeks, see how you like us, and most importantly how the students react to you. It's been really awful for them. After two weeks, if all goes as we think it will, and we are being positive," he paused and swallowed hard, "we will move you from substitute pay to a half year contract. You'd be in the state certified personnel system, with retirement benefits, medical, ability to begin a 401K."

"So the state, what about my credentials?"

"I'm glad you asked; they're giving you emergency credentialing while working on your actual teacher credentialing."

"I absolutely accept; I can do this," Tess smiled to him and nodded.

"At Bellwood I worked with Mrs. Baltimer's third graders for the last two months of the semester because of her illness and recuperation. So I had a little bit of the kind of situation you are describing here. Mrs. Carpenter's students need consistency, a constant cheerful face, knowing that they can learn, and have fun doing it. It sounds as if this's been a really tough experience for these little children."

"That's for sure, and for their parents, also. Parents of these children have become very concerned, the students and their sadness."

"Fourth graders are still young children. We often forget that in the upper primary grades, before middle school."

"I believe you are a fit for our students and our school."

Tess shook hands with Mr. Jameson. Tess wished him a happy holiday season.

"Mrs. Hansler will be your guide, helping you get started with the youngsters."

He handed her the woman's phone number and e-mail address.

Tess left his office and took a quick look down the hall. Teachers' doors were decorated for the holidays. She noted the overall cleanliness and cheerfulness of the building. Earlier, a pleasant office staff woman smiled and brought her coffee. She watched the staff interact with an upset parent as Tess waited to talk with the principal.

"Remember, Tess, this is not Bellwood, a big elementary school in town. This school's small, almost in a rural area near an older part of north Beet City. Faculty and staff wear a lot of hats, I suspect. Wow, kids, these kids need my help."

She whispered that as she walked out of Downing Elementary School. She turned at the curb and looked back.

"I can do this. This will be my new school home."

She clapped and jumped up and down and pounded on her steering wheel after she got in her car. As she drove to Aunt Em's, her mind started swirling.

"Gotta find a home for Beth and me, now look for one, must tell my family."

She put her bags in her bedroom and straight away got a cup of coffee.

Tess stood in front of the Christmas tree.

"Thank you, God, for my life; I can serve you through working with my little ones."

She wrapped her arms around herself and waltzed around the living room.

"This is my wonderful Christmas blessing, to love, to be loved."

After she wrapped two presents and put them under the tree, she headed out the door to pick up Beth.

"Craig," she spoke out, "Craig, it's my time to find you, a fine man who has waited and waited for me to finish."

⁊ↄ

"Thank you for taking this morning off the day before Christmas Eve to come with me."

Tess looked over to Craig and touched his shoulder, "It is my pleasure."

They drove to the small home of Craig's parents on the east outskirts of Beet City. Tess smelled coffee and baking wafting from the kitchen. She and Craig both took off their boots and coats and walked toward the couple sitting at a small table in the breakfast nook.

Brent Huntcrowe stood and walked toward Tess.

"Welcome Tess," he smiled as he shook her hand. "Come meet Coleen; she's having a good day."

Tess shook hands with Craig's mom. She watched the mother nod to her and say Hi.

"It's good to finally meet you," Tess gazed first at Coleen and then Brent.

Everyone sat with coffee and cinnamon rolls which Brent took out of the oven earlier.

"You just graduated, congratulations, Tess," Coleen nodded and gave her a smile.

"Thank you; my mind just whirls around, so much's happened. Craig doesn't know this, but I also will be teaching right away after Christmas."

"Will it be for the Downing Elementary teacher killed in the accident after Halloween?" Brent asked.

Craig saw Tess's eyes widen in surprise, "Oh my goodness, yes, it will be."

Brent added, "We know the family; it was a terrible situation, for the Carpenter family. Two young children left without a mother, and also for the school."

"Those poor children," Coleen added, "They will need you so much, bring some stability to their classroom."

"That's my goal, to bring stability and continual learning. The principal shared about the number of people who've worked with these little kids since the accident."

"So many subs, and staff when there were no subs."

"You know the situation, then, when staff get sick."

"Right," she paused, "years ago, I worked in the kitchen at Downing, know all the ups and downs of a school situation. I have every confidence that you will keep the ship upright, so to speak."

Tess smiled to Craig's mom.

"Yes, very well put."

The four of them finished their rolls and coffee.

"I'll go lie down now. It was so good to meet you, Tess."

Craig and Tess said their goodbyes and left the Huntcrowe home.

"Now we'll head to the farm. What do you think?"

"Your mom, she fixed up for us. Her hair, nice, and a touch of lipstick."

"She's really trying, for the holiday season."

"Each day is precious."

"My sister is cooking and bringing the meal to my parent's home for Christmas day. My brother-in-law and the three nephews will join us. Mom cannot really leave her home. Dad handles all the medication and hospice checks on her twice during the week. We want her last Christmas to be fun, but not upsetting. We'll not exchange presents, just eat, and maybe play a game. The boys are kinda rough, but they love playing games. They know it's not long for their grandma."

"My prayers go out to all of you, Craig, so hard, what you're going through."

Tess started paying attention to the county road they were on. Craig turned in to a well-plowed lane. He pulled over at a break in the fence that ran along both sides of the lane.

"We're hopping out here. There's something I want to show you."

"They held hands as they walked through the snow to a stand of trees. They moved into the trees. Craig stood still in front of a dead tree, broken down a little above its six foot top.

Snow blew in and covered the tree. It stood, with a thick branch sticking out from each side, all covered in white.

"Oh Craig, a cross."

"My Christmas cross, I discovered it several years ago. It looks so awesome now with the sun shining on the cross through the trees in the background. I walk out here now to pray, my own private cathedral."

"Your prayer?"

"The light of God's love, may it bring joy and peace to me and all my loved ones this Christmas."

Craig looked over to Tess. He watched the tears flow from her eyes. She turned to him and they hugged. They held the hug for a long time. She raised her lips to his. They came together, kissing and kissing.

"Together, we can be together," he whispered to her.

"Yes, after all this time, waiting and waiting."

They held hands as they returned to the pickup.

"We're running short on time; I got to get you back to pick up Beth. But I must show you my place, what I've done."

Tess saw the two wings, brought out on the left and right sides of the house. He helped her up the walk and into the home where they took off their boots.

"It's cool, maybe leave your coat on. Here we are, the great room, looking back to the fireplace and windows set to each side of the fireplace."

Tess saw a kitchen and dining area on the left and a small library on the right. Down each hall were two bedrooms with bathrooms nearby.

"The basement is finished, a fifth bedroom or a man cave and a bathroom there, along with the washer and dryer."

"Oh my gosh, Craig, you've done so much."

"I had a lot of help. I used some of the replacement monies from the fire. The rest of the fire money went to pay for the home Mom and Dad live in."

"So you're carrying a small mortgage."

"Yeah, very small now, good crop years, but sometimes the crops don't pan out."

"It's very lovely, Craig, so natural, with all the wood and the magnificent fireplace."

Tess remained very quiet on the way back to her home.

"I have so much to think about, Craig. I need time and space, for Beth and for me. I've been moving along at blinding speed since high school. But I want to continue to see you. You have your mom, and whatever I can do to help you. I saw the hospital bed in the living room and the wonderful Christmas tree."

"Yeah, dad has it set up real nice for her. She sees the lit Christmas tree day and night."

"Does she sleep much at night?"

"Right, the morphine holds her for about five hours. So dad gets to sleep from 11 to 4 a.m. He's surviving. He knows how precious each day is." He shook his head, "One day, mom's lungs will just stop."

They drove the rest of the way in silence. Tess reached across and hugged Craig. She asked to be let out so she could run two errands before picking up Beth.

"I care so much, Tess."

"And I care for you, Craig, Merry Christmas."

"To you also."

They smiled to each other. He watched her walk to Aunt Em's front porch. She turned and waved to him.

≈

"Oh, Happy Day," Marty said. She took Beth from Tess's arms and kissed her.

"Peez, wan down."

"OK, Missy."

Tess shook her head to her mom as her mom put Beth down.

Marty nodded, "She has her own mind."

The little girl looked around the tiny living room with its very small tree.

Beth walked over to the tree and turned, "Petty tree, Grama."

"Thank you, sweet girl."

It hit Tess, "That's what mom always called me, all the time I lived with her."

Aunt Emily, Granddad Joe, and Great Granddad Jack watched the little girl.

"One of us," is all Jack said as he smiled to everyone.

"Mom, it's all delicious."

"I just remember how you helped me with holiday dinners in the past. You were the organized one; me, not so much," Marty giggled.

The family continued to enjoy the meal, folks taking turns holding Beth and feeding her.

"This kid's got an appetite," they all agreed.

"Dad, where's Angela?"

"With her dad's family, also her boy's there to see grandparents."

"And Kyle, Mom?"

"Right, he's with his son and family, but he wishes all of us a Happy Christmas."

"Back at him, please," Granddad Jack nodded to her.

After they ate, they gathered in the living room. This year, for the first time, Tess confirmed it was OK to give Beth a book. Always before, while Beth didn't comprehend about giving, they gave money for her educational savings account. They all agreed to continue that practice.

Beth opened her package carefully.

"Book, a book," she beamed to everyone watching her.

Tess knelt next to her, "Oh Beth, this is a wonderful book, *The Little Engine that Could.*"

She smiled as she looked over to her Dad.

"Granddad Joe read this book to me even when I was tiny."

Joe got down on the floor and sat next to Tess and Beth.

"Before I knew it, Tess read the book to me."

Everyone laughed and clapped.

"Yeah, I loved that book like crazy, a little engine that never gave up."

"Kinda like you, Tess."

She looked up to her Granddad Jack, "Perseverance, yeah, I was sorta that little engine."

"May I read the story to my girls?"

Beth looked up to him and nodded. Tess held Beth on her lap as Granddad Jack moved to the floor.

And so the family heard Jack read the story of the little engine who through hard work accomplished what he set out to do. He pointed out pictures as he went along in his reading.

"That was wonderful," Marty spoke out once Jack finished.

The family clapped, "Thank you, Granddad Jack."

Tess put Beth down in the spare bedroom, her old room. She settled down and closed her eyes right away. Tess looked around, old memories bombarding her from days past. Her mom transformed the space into a simple quiet bedroom. Tess saw that her mom painted the paneling in the bedroom a pale blue and changed out the curtains and bedspread. She noticed the new flooring installed throughout the trailer. Tess thought at first that wood floors got installed, but on further inspection she realized the surface was vinyl.

"My," she blew out a breath, "mom's done a lot with this place; she musta convinced the landlord it would be worth it for the next renter, charging a higher rent."

Everyone got pumpkin pie, whipped topping and coffee after Joe and Emily cleaned up the dishes.

"Mom, you did yourself proud, with your efforts today," Tess smiled to her mom.

"It was my pleasure; it's much easier since you showed me how to get organized and do a little bit at a time."

"Everyone, please keep Craig and his family in your prayers. His mom, Coleen, has little time left. Morphine helps ease her discomfort, her failing lungs. She so wanted to be with her family through Christmas, and maybe into the New Year."

"We will pray, Tess," Aunt Em said.

"Yes, we all will pray for her to soon arrive at her eternal peace, and strength for the family after she's gone," Granddad Jack added.

"What is the family doing?"

"Craig's sister is cooking a Christmas noon meal and bringing it. She and her husband have three sons, active boys. They'll all eat together, no gift exchange, but sharing of Christmases past. Then Coleen must rest and they'll leave."

"Hospice?"

"Oh yes, they'll start coming daily after the first of the year. It's so hard right now; people in health care, they also deserve to have holiday celebrations."

Before her dad left, Tess pulled him aside.

"How's Ethan, his family?"

"They're all busy, but he sent me a Christmas card. He wrote in it that he wanted to continue to see you, me, and Beth. And he again praised you for your efforts in bringing us all together."

"That completely can happen. I'll be moving to my own place, I hope by early February. I gotta have a paycheck so I can pay rent. Everyone's helped me through the years.

"Uh huh, time to stand up on your own two feet, found something?"

"Yip, two prospects, I feel lucky because we've got two colleges in Beet City. So there's not a lot available."

Once Beth woke from her nap she and Tess left Farnon for Aunt Em's in Beet City. Beth held her new book the whole trip.

"Are you looking at the pictures of the engine?"

"Yes, Mommy."

"It's a great book which you'll read to me before you know it. You'll recognize the words."

Tess and Beth sang "Silent Night" as they approached their home. Tess looked around, admiring the pristine snow and bright sunshine as she and Beth arrived.

"Thank you, God, for my little girl, for my life, and this beautiful day. Take me and guide me in Your way."

ஃ

"I hope you had a Happy Christmas, Tess."

"I did, share about your day and what you've been doing; it's soon to be New Year's Eve. This wondrous and difficult year, it's almost come to an end."

Tess sat at the kitchen island holding the phone.

"Christmas Day, it was so pleasant, mom having a good day, my nephews and my sis and brother-in-law, all in good spirits. But dad, he's really struggling. The care giver, closest survivor, he's got so much he's got to do, especially when she leaves all of us."

"Have you helped him?"

"Right, the funeral's all planned at the mortuary, with a reception right after in the same facility. She's chosen cremation, has her short obituary written and chose her gravestone, already installed at Longpoint. My mom, always a super organized person, always worked away from the farm."

"She made her own life, but still supported your dad in his work, the farm."

"That's pretty much it, that is, until the fire. Everything changed. She's never seen the new home, mine now, at the same location after the fire. But that's OK, she says, her new memories of their home in town, she's embraced the newness."

"Will your dad stay in the home in town?"

"Yeah, for now, he still loves the farm, as I've mentioned in the past, he likes to come and help out."

"So the Palmersts met at my mom's place in Farnon. Dad, Beth, Granddad Jack, and Aunt Emily joined in the delicious meal. We're not gift givers, but there was one present, for Beth, a book. I've decided that family can give her books, but that's all."

"Really?"

"The family contributes money for her education?"

"Set up in a savings account?"

"Yeah, which I'll convert to a Certificate of Deposit, but I'll wait until it's over a $1,000."

"Good for you, Tess. You can imagine the cost of your daughter's education in 16 years."

"Uh huh, hard to comprehend, I doubt she'll have the support I had, my Aunt Em and dad."

"If she's super smart, there'll be scholarships."

"Right, Craig, how're you doing, emotionally?"

"Very hard, I'm up and down, and I know I will be for a while after she's actually gone."

"Please try to get enough sleep, eat nutritious stuff, exercise," she paused, "your dad's gonna need you, big time."

"I know, I think we're as ready as we can be. God wants her to spend a little more time on earth. What we do now is read to her a little. She's pretty much sleeping."

"New Year's Eve?"

"I'll spend it with mom and dad; we'll have a champagne toast early and then she'll sleep into the new year."

"I'll be with Aunt Em, my last holiday time with her. She has several single teacher friends. We'll all be together for snacks and lots of sparkling cider. None of them drink alcohol when they're driving."

"Your life's gonna change, big time."

"Did I tell you, uh, nah, we haven't talked in a bit. Dad gave me a loan for my first and last month's rent. I found my place for Beth and me; we move in January 15. I told dad I'd pay him back by March."

"Child care center and your new school, close or far away from your new home?"

"Child care's furthest, then school, I can't complain. The place's got new carpet, vinyl, all new paint and updated appliances, kinda looks like it took a beating before me. Bathroom's not clean, but I'm a white-glove neat nick."

"You'll whip it into shape."

"I'm most concerned about my fourth graders; I can't meet with the person advising me until an hour before classes start after the new year."

"Can you even get into the building?"

"Right, for one morning, the school secretary'll be there, doing mail and catch up. I'll have three hours; I can't even imagine what I'll face."

"Hope for the best; expect the worst."

"Oh my gosh, Craig, that is exactly what I just thought."

&

"Your keys, Miss Palmerst," the school secretary handed them to her.

"Thanks, I'm anxious to get in there; I've created a few things for the board and wall. I haven't seen the room. If I need to, where to put trash; I brought several bags?"

She passed the janitor's area so knew where trash went. Tess tried the key to open her classroom door. The door wouldn't budge.

"Great," she blew out a breath, "I don't have a lot of time."

She looked at the door frame and the door knob. She pulled the door toward her and tried the lock.

"Joy, oh Joy, I've unlocked my classroom."

Two hours later Tess felt her head pounding.

"I've done what I can; things are in better order. I start fresh with my students. I completely rearranged the room, with a reading circle area in one corner, and a small group work area in the other corner. Students' first names are on the corner of the desk. Thank goodness I at least have their names. 19, 19 is just a great number to work with. I consider myself lucky, six tables with three students each, plus one student alone for now," she spoke out.

She remembered her class during her internship; she made at least five seating changes while she worked with the students. At the end she felt she had the correct students sitting with other students who would help propel the students forward in their studies. Tess knew she had five good leaders in that class. And she always had one kid who needed to be alone to concentrate. She wasn't sure what would happen here.

"Tess, don't second guess; these are different kids; some from the countryside, but with parents who really care. Try to remember what they've been through the last two months. It's called being devastated," she whispered.

For her final task, she cleared her outside classroom door of several paper ornaments the students made. Tess did not see names or ownership on the ornaments so she put them in a stack of items she would talk about with her students.

"This is, for sure, not the look of the classroom they walked out of in December. But, kids, we'll do this. You all have so much to learn, 'cause next year, it's your last before moving to middle school."

She stood in front of her closed classroom door. Tess put her hand on the door, "God, please help me with these children. Make their school experience a positive one this semester, thank you," she spoke out.

℅

"We've just about done it, sweet girl."

"Yes, Dad, we have. Without your pickup, and the furniture you gave us, well."

"It was our pleasure," Joe added quickly.

"You and Angela gave me nice stuff, a double bed for me and a twin bed for Beth."

"They sat in our basement, when we made decisions about what to change in the home. Both the double bed and twin bed mattresses are new. The underneath pieces and frames are old."

"Plus Aunt Em donated a couch she doesn't want any more. So I have a piece of living room furniture."

Joe smiled to his daughter and hugged her.

"I have no doubt that other pieces will appear."

"I'm OK now; I found the circle table and four chairs, at the resale store, my very first purchase."

℅

"Three weeks into this semester, this spring 2004, and I think I am beginning to understand my students," Tess spoke out as she drove from Downing Elementary to pick up Beth.

They sang on the way to their home. "Dashing Through the Snow" remained Beth's choice after many months of singing Christmas carols.

"Aunty Em, when?" Beth asked.

"We'll see her on Sunday, after church. She's coming over for Sunday dinner. She'll be our first guest having dinner in our home."

"Mommy will sing, at church?"

"I will, sweet girl."

"I go to Sunay school."

Tess got out and opened the garage door. They drove in and gathered their backpacks and bags. As they always had, they took their own stuff to their own bedrooms.

Beth knew that her mom hated a mess and that her mom needed help around their home. So she did help.

"Mommy's a teacher," Beth always said with pride in her voice. "Help at home, help pre-school."

Tess felt a sweet flutter of satisfaction in herself that her daughter talked like that about her.

"She's a fine little one," Tess nodded as she stepped out into the hall and peeked for a moment into Beth's bedroom.

Together they fixed up Beth's room, the little bit that they could in a rental.

Beth had a pale blue rug to step on when she got out of bed. a pale blue bedspread and matching curtains at the window. The little girl had a bookcase that held the books she started getting from family. The rest of the shelf held the numerous books Beth got from the library. Every Saturday Beth carried some of her books back into the Beet City Library. Her mom helped with all the other books they read together through the week.

∞

"Tess, I needed to call you. Mom's gone, her pain over, peace at last."

"Craig, I am so sorry. Stay strong, for your dad, for you, for your sister and family, and all the other Huntcrowe family. Beth's asleep, talk to me, what can I do to help out?"

"Could you come to mom's reception after the funeral? Don't know if I mentioned it, but the funeral's in one section of the mortuary and the catered reception will be in the large reception area, same location. It's the way mom wanted it, no fuss or muss for the family. And the mortuary staff will take care of the burial of her cremains; we won't attend that. Dad, well, it's about all he can handle now."

"I understand; he's got the reading of the will and also other decisions to make. I remember, I wasn't very old, but I helped out some when my grandma died years back. My granddad liked having me there, perked him up as he went along on his way to becoming a single person again. He sought my opinion on several things about grandma. We sorted through her clothes and all her other personal things. She had some nice stuff; I convinced him that he should give her things to a nonprofit which helped out needy folks. My mom used to buy our clothes from a second-hand store."

"How did that go, giving her things away?"

"Granddad Jack felt grateful that he did all that. He didn't seem to have an emotional attachment to her stuff. So many people needed, still need all kinds of help. I know my mom and I did, after I moved in with her. The memories of my grandma, pretty mixed for granddad. I will share sometime what I mean by that."

"So you'll come? It'll be on Saturday, when more working folks may be able to attend."

"I'm sure Aunt Em can help me with Beth, so I'll say yes."

"Tess, I miss you so much; it's just devastating watching someone just fade to death."

"And I miss you, Craig. You and your family are in my thoughts and prayers. Especially you and your dad, you survivors, you have to go on, continue living, loving, and one day enjoying this bright wonderful world that's out there."

Tess felt a burn in her stomach, a pain she had not felt since she lost her family. She took a deep breath and got the time and location. She put the information on her daily calendar she kept tucked away in her kitchen.

"Whew, I gotta stay super-organized," she said as she felt Beth at her side. She picked her daughter up and hugged her.

"Whatcha want for dinner?"

"Mac and cheese," was Beth's standard answer.

Tess decided her daughter probably could eat that meal almost every day. Now they worked on adding more green vegetables to both their diets. Tess realized she never ate nutritious meals with her mom. She started changing that when she moved in with Aunt Em.

ॐ

Tess arrived at the mortuary. She looked around and heard the quiet of the empty area. She found her way into a room with lots of folks milling about, talking to each other. But she could not understand some of what they spoke. And she heard a beautiful melody. She caught sight of a man blowing into a Native American flute, creating a song harkening back to a past time. She stopped and moved to the side of the room where the flutist played. Tess listened to the haunting melody. And then she really noticed it. Almost everyone had black hair, many of the men with long hair tied back. And some were dressed in outfits that looked like they had an Indian origin. Some of the women wore soft leather moccasins on their feet.

Tess searched the room for Craig and for his dad, Brent. She nodded her head as it came to her. These folks are Native American, maybe from the reservation?

She watched as Craig caught her eye. He waved to her. She waved back and made her way through the folks conversing in the room.

"Thank you for coming. This's so much harder than I ever imagined it would be."

She shuddered as she saw his red-veined eyes.

"Craig, let's get something to eat."

"That's a good idea; it's been a long time since breakfast. And I haven't drunk anything either."

She steered him to the table filled with snacks, cookies, and several desserts.

"Mom wanted lots of sweets; do you think this is enough sugar for this crew?"

Craig smiled to her. Tears filled her eyes as she nodded to him.

"He's still got his sense of humor, I'm so glad."

"What were you just thinking?"

"Humor, you've still got your sense of humor, so neat that's what your mom requested."

She carried the two cups of coffee to a table where a couple sat. Craig followed her with two plates filled with snacks. After they set their food down, Craig introduced the couple to Tess.

"These are my aunt and uncle, Sadie and George Huntcrowe."

His uncle stood and shook hands with Tess. Sadie continued to sit and held out her hand to Tess. Craig expressed his thanks that they came to support Brent. Tess realized it then; this is a Native American family. George's long black hair went to his waist. He tied it back. And Sadie braided her thick black hair into two braids. Craig never shared about his parents' families.

"I know Craig's concern remained to help his mom as long as he could and now to comfort and support his dad," Tess shared with this couple.

Tess listened as Craig spoke to his uncle about what seemed to be in the future for Brent and the farm. And she learned an important Huntcrowe situation. From what she heard from the conversation, Craig's granddad decided to leave the reservation, the home of the Apsaalooke tribe. He came to work on the farm of James Cochran, outside Beet City after his high school graduation. This granddad helped, did such a good job, that when James Cochran, a bachelor, knew he was going to die, he deeded the land and homestead to Craig's granddad, Johnny.

George and Sadie wished Craig well in his continued farming pursuits.

"I want to invite you to my home, see my place, and I'll have dad come out so we can have a meal together."

"Thank you, Craig, we really want to get to know you better, your dad."

"Right," Craig nodded to his aunt and uncle, "Dad wasn't social. But I wanted to let you know that the Great Spirit is with me, with dad, with all of us, as we honor mom."

Tess watched his aunt and uncle smile to him and nod.

Later Craig and Tess found his dad. Tess hugged Brent and told him she would continue to pray special prayers for him and the family.

"We're the survivors, sometimes people forget about us," he said as Tess stepped away from him.

"Your family cares, Brent, you're lucky to have a son and a daughter who will be in this area. Craig, for sure, with the farm, I know you can count on him."

"For sure, I will be able to have their emotional support. And I do have my family, George and Leo, my brothers, and my sister, Lily."

"And, Dad, other friends, from the reservation," Craig added.

Tess said goodbye to Brent, and Craig held her hand as they walked across the room.

"I will leave now, Craig."

"Thank you so much for coming; if I may, I'd like to drop by this evening. There's so much about me that you have no knowledge of; you had a glimpse of all that at the reception."

"It will be good to get away from all family things, at your dad's and your own home, all those memories, just for a little while."

"Amen," he took a deep breath, "I'll come by about 8 p.m. I know you and Beth have church in the morning."

"Yes, every Sunday that we can. I love singing in our little choir, and Beth's in Sunday school. She says she talks to God there."

ℰℭ

Craig did come by, right at 8 p.m. They hugged. Tess took his coat and lay it over a living room chair.

"Wow, sure looks different from when I peeked in as you were moving in."

"My first home, Beth and I have it fixed up the way we want. She's very young, but she already has definite opinions on a lot of things, especially how she looks, her clothes, her room, and she's emphatic about what she cares about."

"And that is?"

"Love, she loves me, all the family, she checks on me, asks, 'Mommy, happy?'"

"Whew, hope she never loses that."

"She won't if I have anything to say about it."

"You're a super caring mom."

"I am, but I'll not be a hover mom; I see that a little bit with my own students, their folks," Tess shook her head to him.

"Come sit at the dining room table. Here's your coffee, yeah, I know, you drink it day and night."

"I told you that?"

"Right, and I know you like pie. Beth and I created this cherry pie in celebration of Valentine's Day, coming up."

"But you'll share with me?"

"Course," she smiled to him as she set a generous piece of pie, a fork and a napkin in front of him. She brought her own piece to the table and sat down next to him at the circle table.

She watched him nod to her, "It feels so comforting, to be in your presence, Tess. I bet your kids feel it."

"I try to have the light of love, to project that, to those little ones around me."

"You do, you project that light with me, right now."

He took his left hand and touched her cheek.

"You don't know about this, but I took a chance, after I'd been with my students three weeks. They write every day in their journals, free flow, whatever they want. Some of them write pretty awesome stuff, have a couple of poets in my group. Anyway, one day a student mentioned Mrs. Carpenter.

Another student spoke up, "Miss Palmerst, can we write today, maybe write to Mrs. Carpenter, tell her what we've been doing."

"Do you think she looks down at us from heaven?" another student asked.

"Class, what do you think?" I asked my group.

I watched many students nod their heads.

"Please, go ahead."

She smiled to Craig as tears came to her eyes.

"That day I gave the class a little longer to write. After they finished, my kids and I talked about losing their teacher. Kids shared about loss, a family member, a pet, losing a game they played. They all put away their journals and agreed that they needed to get on with their school day, that it would be what Mrs. Carpenter would want."

"Wow, I guess I don't remember being sensitive like that to loss. Well, yeah, when we lost our home, burning down, that stands out. But that's a wonderful story you shared."

He brought his plate to the sink and poured himself more coffee.

"Let's move to the couch; thanks to Aunt Em I have it."

"It fits well with your tan carpeting."

They drank coffee and set their cups on the corner table with its lamp.

He turned to her. The shine of his dusky gray eyes shone into hers, warming her.

"I love you, Tess."

"And I love you, Craig. I have, for a very long time, but," and she stopped.

He nodded to her, "But it's taken until now."

"That's right, I had life, an education, a daughter, all interconnected."

"I know that. I've loved you since I saw you with your head down, at the table at the cc where we sat that first semester you were there. Concern, and a leap of my heart, I knew you were the one."

"Where did you gather all the patience through those years?"

"From God, who kept telling me to care for you, that one day," he paused.

"That one day," she started.

Craig turned to her, touched her lips, and they kissed. Soft, caressing kisses became French kisses, tongue to tongue, teasing and teasing. She touched his chest as he kissed her neck. They kissed, now in time freely, without any more wondering.

They stopped, catching their breath. She snuggled into his neck.

"I'm home, in his loving arms," Tess thought. "I'm sharing my last thought, Craig, I'm home, in your loving arms."

"You are."

They sat together for a time, in the quiet of her home.

"About the reception, I never told you anything about my family."

"I certainly saw a group of caring folks there, checking in with your dad. There were smiles, and the flute player, that was an awesome touch."

"Mom used to play that flute; so the music, sure enough, was in memory of her, Dad requested it."

"And I saw folks spend a few moments with you and with your sister."

"Although I don't look it that much, I am Native American, from the Apsaalooke tribe."

"Your eyes, dusky gray, and skin tone, you're lighter-skinned than almost everyone else I saw at the reception. I just assumed your dad had his tan from years of working outside."

"Well, we had a white woman, a great grandmother, or something, so that's where I picked up the gray eyes. Mom and Dad both have brown eyes, my sister, same dark eyes."

"I have a somewhat same eye color situation in my family. I'll be sharing that with you one day. Suffice it to say, my folks both have blue eyes, my mom's especially fabulous eyes."

"Well, I've never met anyone with eyes the color of yours."

"Yeah, folks tell me that."

"You are beautiful, and I know I'm not the only one who could drown in those glorious blue eyes."

She nodded and smiled to him. She started to color up, her face changing from pale to a bright rose color.

"You don't take compliments well."

"No, Craig, I don't. I'm just me."

"I was unable to celebrate Valentine's Day, so close after Mom's death."

"Well, you must. What do you propose?"

"I would like to invite you and Beth to my home for a post-Valentine, pre-Easter lunch on a Saturday. Please check your calendar."

"You cook?"

"I do, and I'm a pretty darn good cook."

"You'll have to figure what I can contribute to the celebration."

"Pie, whatever kind you and Beth enjoy."

They set the day and time.

Craig rose from the couch after they kissed again.

"Tess," he looked down at her, "I can't, can't do any more loving with you right now, everything."

She got up and stood next to him, "It's all too much, you need time. You gave me so much time. I must give you time now."

"Thanks for that, Tess. I'm emotionally a mess, need to sort out the family stuff, and then go on. I want to go on with you."

She hugged him and whispered in his ear, "As I want to go on with you."

He kissed her on the forehead, "Thank you for being with me; it was heartfelt."

❧

And because of a big snowstorm, the lunch got postponed.

"Mind if I bring an older guy guest to lunch with us?"

"Course, I always fix more than we can eat."

And so Ethan joined Tess and Beth for the lunch at Craig's home.

"Craig, I'd like you to meet Ethan Overridge."

They shook hands.

Beth walked hand in hand with her mom through the great room to the kitchen. Tess set the foil-covered cherry pie on a counter away from the main cooking area.

"Sir, I had a bit of a shock when I saw you standing in the great room, as you gazed around at the area."

"Please call me Ethan, and yes, folks are shocked, as was I when I first learned of this family situation."

"You're really a bit older version of your son, 'course I've only seen pictures of Joe."

"Craig hasn't met my parents. That's next for me, to introduce the three of them."

"We'll share the story, after lunch. Beth's hungry."

"Want to try a chair, Beth?"

She nodded and patted the chair with the books piled up to allow her to eat with them.

"See, no high chair, big girl now," she smiled to her mom, then turned and nodded to Ethan and Craig.

"We're having a picnic lunch, but inside."

"It's cole outside," Beth said to Craig.

They ate the buffalo burgers, potato chips, and raw carrots.

"It's all delicious, Craig, our compliments to the chef," Ethan spoke out.

Beth, Tess, and he clapped for Craig's efforts.

"Pie now, peez."

"OK, then you'll lie down for a rest."

Beth nodded her head to her mom, "I know, Mommy."

Tess warmed the pieces of cherry pie, and asked who wanted vanilla ice cream over the top.

"Dewishous," Beth smiled to everyone.

"Wow, you finished your pie first. I enjoyed it also, sweet great-granddaughter."

"Go rest," she spoke to her mom.

Craig showed them to a small bedroom on the right wing of the home. After Beth got comfortable on the twin bed he placed a blanket over her. Tess kissed her on the forehead. As they left, Craig took her hand, raised it to his own, and kissed it. They walked hand in hand back into the great room. While they tended Beth, Ethan poured more coffee into their mugs and set them down on the side table near the fireplace.

Craig started the gas fireplace and they sat near each other, Craig and Tess on the couch facing the fireplace. Ethan sat in a comfortable chair nearby.

"Help me understand what's going on here?" Craig asked.

"Tess is my biological granddaughter. Her dad, Joe, is my son."

"Oh my," Craig blew out a big breath and took a drink of his coffee.

"Tess, go ahead. You are the person responsible of reconnecting the family."

"So, Craig," she took a deep breath and began, "Ethan loved my grandma, Donna. Yeah, I know, he and Donna fell in love during a very down time in their early marriages. He was a new lawyer in the county. Grandma worked for the sheriff's office, administrative work in that county. That's how they met."

"We loved each other for one fall, broke it off at Christmas that year. We weighed everything and decided to remain in our relationships, me with Holly, and Donna with Jack. Oh my dear God," Ethan's voice broke, "I loved her, beyond life, then, now, and always will. There's a place in my heart where Donna'll remain. Maybe one day in heaven, well," he held his throat as tears formed in his eyes.

"And, then?"

"The next August," Tess said, "my dad, Joe was born. And at almost the same time Ethan and Holly had a son, David."

"And with the healing of having a son, Holly grew back into a loving relationship with me."

"Now I gotta know. How did you two find each other?"

"Through my granddad, Jack, Joe's dad. I'm throwing around a lot of names. On her deathbed Grandma Donna asked Granddad Jack to give a man named Ethan Overridge a letter. And then she told Jack that Joe was the biological son to Ethan."

Craig put his head in his hands and stayed quiet.

"So, granddad asked me to try to find this Ethan Overridge, to give him the letter Donna requested him to have. Granddad seemed real distraught over the news. He got some help and reexamined his earlier life."

"And Tess found out who I was, after a time of searching."

"Yeah, it was almost time for Beth's birth. I gave the letter to a staff member in the county where Ethan held a judgeship. He got the letter."

"Horrible shock, angry, at first with Donna, for never sharing that I had a son with her. Uh huh, I got counseling, a minister helped me. After some time I got in contact with Jack Palmerst, your granddad."

"And eventually my dad learned the truth of his parentage."

Craig shook his head, "Your dad, Joe, he musta been so shocked."

"Yeah, he was, but when he finally met you, Ethan, it answered questions Joe always had. He's got blue eyes and blonde hair, and looks like a younger you.

I always questioned how Joe got the blue eyes, 'cause both my grandparents had dark brown eyes, and granddad with black hair. I've always been interested in genetics, what we inherited from our past family, especially health situations."

"Make sense?" Ethan gazed at Craig.

"Yeah, it makes sense, a family finding each other. Do you see Joe?"

"We try to get together for lunch every couple of months. But I'm interested in you, Tess, my granddaughter, and Beth, my great granddaughter. I have a bigger family than I ever imagined."

"What are your long-term plans, Ethan?"

"I hope to remain the County Judge of Medi County. No one wants the job, so far, but me. My son, David, and his family live in Alabama, are doing well. It is a pleasure to have family nearby, especially Tess and Beth."

"You are a lucky man, probably what's happened is beyond your wildest expectations, to have these ladies in your world."

"Yes, I have a grandson, some younger, so this is a welcome in my world. My Donna, I talk to her often, she's a light, always remaining in my life. And you, Tess, your incredible eyes, I see a light shining in them, a piece of your grandma."

"Oh Ethan, how wonderful," she spoke out, lowered her head and cried.

"Unbelievable, a family finds each other. You'll share that with Beth when she's older."

"I certainly will, Craig, and thanks for listening to this. I've wanted to share what's happened to us, but it wasn't until now, until you could meet Granddad Ethan, that I felt comfortable relating the story."

"A lot of folks let go of anger and sadness, they let go and let God enter their lives, to soothe them."

"I could never have put it that clearly, Craig," Ethan nodded to him.

"Let me show you around my place, let you know how this all came about for me."

"I'll stay inside, waiting for Beth to wake up. It'll give you two a little time together."

"I will remain, long term it looks like, as the judge of Medi County. And you," he turned and looked at Craig, "have this farm, sugar beets, wheat, barley, that's passed from your dad."

"That's correct."

"The tax implications, what about your sister? Sorry, I'm a lawyer, you've worked this all out?"

"Yes sir, done due diligence."

"That's good to know, you've obviously sought help with your situation."

"I'll show you out back; we'll stand here. I don't want you to have to trudge around in the snow."

Craig pointed out the large barn, set back away from the home, with a corral in back of that. He moved his arm to the right and back where all the Huntcrowe land lay, now in the December snow.

"Our fields remain next to each other, so I plant hundreds of acres that are relatively nearby."

"You are such a lucky family."

"Yes, my granddad, John Huntcrowe, certainly understood that. It's what happens when a person is loyal to an employer, gives his all for the land, for the employer, without thinking of his own future."

"Tess shared," Ethan touched Craig's shoulder, "your mom."

"Right, I chat with her often. I'm worried about dad; theirs was a beautiful relationship, Brent and Coleen. She grew up on the reservation not far from here. But she got to attend high school in Beet City. It's where she met dad."

"And one day, maybe there may be someone else in your dad's life."

"Can't think about that yet, but dad's still in his 50's, so that's a possibility."

"And again, I'm a lawyer, anything I can do to assist you, your dad?"

"My dad's been really on top of the whole situation. And his lawyer's done a super job of getting us all ready for losing her."

"I'm glad, sounds like everyone is moving on. Please, let's get back in. I need to get Tess and Beth headed home; I've still got a drive."

"Right."

"Sure happy I decided to come," he smiled to Craig. "It helps me answer some questions I had about Tess, and about you."

As they returned to the kitchen, "Thank you for your concern about your granddaughter, having two gramps."

Craig looked at Ethan and nodded, "ah, lucky lady."

Ethan laughed with Craig.

Tess hugged her granddad before he left.

"We'll stay in touch."

"Yes, we will, Tess, best of luck with your students, the rest of this year. And I wish you well if you decide you like the school and want to stay on."

"Yes, with a full-year contract."

"We can only hope."

After Beth's nap, Tess and her daughter said their goodbyes to Craig.

"She's the one, my love, we'll get to know each other better," he whispered, as he watched her drive away.

He saw Beth wave to him from the back seat. He waved back to her.

"A little one, gee, she'll be in pre-K before we know it. I've got to start thinking about a little girl in my life. She does have a biological father who pays child support for her," he thought as he wrestled with this extra aspect of his relationship with Tess. He returned inside to clean up the kitchen. For the near future he would concentrate on helping his dad move on, for himself to move on after his mom.

"Snow, Mommy."

"I see that, sweet girl. We don't have far to go."

"Big snowflakes."

"We'll play out in the snow tomorrow, in the big snowflakes, Beth, after church and lunch."

"Play in snow, yay."

Tess heard the jiggling in her daughter's voice and smiled.

"Then the snow, it'll disappear."

"Yes Mommy, fowers come then."

5

"It's planting time, at Craig's home. His fields, he needs to get them ready."

"Planted fowers. Mommy, what's he plant?"

"His main crop is sugar beets, some barley, that's a grain, and he hasn't decided if he's planting wheat."

"Wheat's, grain?"

"Yes, Beth, it is. So Craig is very busy for a few weeks."

"Then everything grows."

"That's right, moisture and good soil, and fertilizer, and sunlight, that's the ticket to good crops."

It was an April Sunday early afternoon. Craig invited them out after church so they could see the planting operation. Tess brought sandwiches, chips, and chocolate chip bars for dessert.

The sun warmed the three of them as they sat in the backyard with their jackets on.

"I'm starved, so let's dig in."

Tess saw his hungry smile.

Beth chose a PB&J, Craig had one ham and one turkey sandwich. Tess had both ham and turkey in her sandwich.

"Your food, it always tastes so delicious to me," Craig nodded to Tess.

"Yeah, that's 'cause you didn't have to fix it."

"Right."

Once they finished Craig gave them a short tour of his planting efforts.

"Sugar beets close to house, why?"

"Because, Beth, that way I can keep an eye on how the growing goes. I have lots of other sugar beet fields."

"Sugar beet farmer?"

"You got it; sugar beets."

"Canee taste sweet, to the beet."

Craig picked up Beth and spoke to her, "You are really smart, knowing that sugar beets can become sugar, for candy. Say, how old are you, really?"

"'Bout 10."

Tess and Craig laughed and laughed.

"So, who told you that?"

"Gran Efan, Grama Marty."

They returned inside so Beth could rest. She closed her eyes after Tess kissed her forehead. Tess poured more coffee for them. Craig and Tess sat next to each other at the island that straddled the midsection of the kitchen. They looked out the windows, one on each side of the fireplace, the focal point of the great room. Tess watched bare trees shake back and forth in the back yard.

"They asked me to return to Downing next fall. I'm going back, taking a fifth grade assignment."

"Contract?"

"Yes, I will have one. It's verbal now. And it looks like I will have many of my students."

"With you since you took over Mrs. Carpenter class?"

"Right."

"The fifth grade teacher's moving to part-time counselor, and other administrative duties."

"Bother you that you know them well?"

"Not at all, we can work together on their strengths and the stuff they're needing help with."

Craig took her hand and kissed it. He turned in his chair to her.

"Your encouragement at mom's death, helping me get through all that sadness, madness. I feel gladness, right now, with you sitting next to me. I love you, Tess."

"I love you, Craig. I appreciate how you've kinda watched over me these past years, accepting me as I am. Your acceptance, encouraging me to move forward. You have so much patience with me."

She choked up, as tears came to her eyes.

"I want to be with you, now, and as we grow old together. Marry me, Tess."

He watched her nod and wide smile.

"Yes, I will marry you, Craig."

They stood and moved away from their chairs. They embraced and kissed. She felt his lips, feather light on hers. She kissed him back. They took a step back from each other as they saw tears, now in both sets of eyes.

"Christmas, Tess, what about Christmas of 2004?"

"Wonderful, a Christmas wedding, our lives joining together. A new beginning for us, at the Christ Child's birth."

"Our daughter," Craig smiled, "ours, a beautiful child."

"Yes, Craig, Beth's young, you'll be the only dad she'll know, a ready-made family," she paused, "uh."

Craig nodded, "We've talked about this, Tess, it's what I want, and a child of our own, one day."

"Yes, our love, an expression of our love."

"This's not like in the movies; I have no ring for you."

"That's 'cause I mentioned once that all I want is a wide gold band, a circle of our love, on my finger for all my life."

They hugged and held hands as they walked to the tall window to the left of the fireplace.

"Oh Craig, you remembered about the ring."

"I listen carefully to what you have to say, dear one."

৪০

In early October the sugar beets ripened for picking. Craig cut his wheat, barley, and soy beans earlier. He had a good report.

This year the sucrose percentage of the sugar beets turned out to be excellent.

"That's the news I have, Tess, I am so happy with how the processing went after the picking. "

"So, the sucrose determines the value of the crop?"

"Exactly, processing doesn't happen immediately, 'cause it's now late November. But I'm good with the determination."

"So your year has been?"

"Fine, and I'm so excited, our wedding coming up. But I know you got lots going on."

"The biggest surprise, for all of us faculty, was the decision to combine two small fifth grades and two small third grades. So my group of 15 became a larger group of 25. We lost some students in those two grades, moved away. Changes had to be made. I've adjusted to my 25. I knew my 15, so I had only 10 new students to become acquainted with. I've been pleased with my previous students, how they adjusted to the change. Kids are super adaptable."

They stood together on Craig's back patio.

"We've started planning our day. Keep your thoughts about what we want to have."

"I will, dear one. I'm so pleased your year's going so positive with your students."

℘

This year the assignment of the Christmas production for the elementary school went to Tess. It was a dream she had all throughout her training for becoming a teacher. And she understood now how the two music classes she took as a student would help her.

"What do you think?" she asked her class after they talked about ideas for the program mid-semester.

"We can do this, Miss Palmerst."

"How about a sleigh and bells? We could make a small sleigh, have the image of a horse pulling the sleigh. What about songs?"

Students threw out ideas, deciding on "Dashing Through the Snow" and "Sleigh Bells Ring." The songs fit with the objects Tess helped them decide to be part of the stage presentation.

"I have one request."

"Tell us, Miss Palmerst."

"I would like to end the program with a song called "Bells.""

"I hear the bells....the morning," she sang to them.

"Try it with me."

The students picked up the melody and soon had the words, repeating a sentence and then adding a couple of words.

"Miss Palmerst, it's so lovely. I've never heard it."

Many of the class shook their heads, "Neither have we."

"Let's sing it again," a student suggested.

"Stand?"

Tess raised her hands. The students stood and raised their voices, now catching the tune and the words.

They sat down and clapped their hands. Tess saw smiles all around.

"We need a story to go with the songs, right Miss Palmerst?"

"I have two thoughts."

They looked to her, "Song, then a little play on stage, then second song, then a little play on stage."

"Finish with "Bells?""

"Can do, then maybe a tiny little action on stage, then do bells song one last time."

"That's a super idea, Sara. Let's think on it tonight, and then tomorrow, during morning writing time, we'll work further."

"Our own production, from us fifth graders to the school."

"Exactly, Luke, and we must figure out how to include students from other grades."

"Singing," she heard from her students.

"Yeah, learn the song during music class, that we have once a week."

"Uh huh, if our traveling music teacher will let us."

"Thank you, for that, Julia, I'll find out right away, so we don't do unnecessary work." The next day Tess came back with news.

"Our principal approved our idea, and the music teacher will work with classes. She'll get the words to the songs for the students in grades one through four. Don't you think a lot of students will know "Dashing" and "Sleigh Bells Ring?"

"They will, or can learn them quick, but "Bells", it's beautiful but it'll be a new song for many younger students, like it is for some of us," Stephanie spoke out.

"So, are we ready to begin?"

She saw nods from the students. Tess divided the class into three groups, each charged with writing out a particular song and working with the song words to figure out an act, with the same characters and props for all three songs. She had all the students write out the words to "Bells."

"At the end we will all sing "Bells.""

"That's nice, Miss Palmerst, all the grades are included. It'll be enough participation from the younger students."

"Yeah, Stephanie, so that the parents will be satisfied," another student spoke up.

"We can only work on this during writing time, but I'll give you a little more time each day, until we have all of this under control."

Over the next weeks the class wrote out the three small acts, starting with the song. Soon they set aside a part of the classroom as a stage and proceeded to begin the acting. Only students who wanted to do the acting got asked. Other students in the class offered to help with other aspects of the production.

"We're kinda stuck on the sleigh," Tess mentioned to Craig when she and her students came to the play props for the program.

"I got this," he smiled to her.

One Sunday afternoon he met Tess at her classroom. He built a side of a sleigh, with boards to help it stand up. A red sheet he dyed covered the sleigh side. Three small chairs sat inside the sleigh, just enough room for two riders in the back seat and one driver for the horse. One fifth grader consented to be the horse. The sleigh would be moved out of the classroom on its side and placed on the stage, when practices started there. Craig made certain of that. He and Tess moved the sleigh out of the room and down the hall, as a trial transfer before the actual transfer to the gym stage.

"This's gonna work out super good," Craig hugged her after they brought the sleigh back in the room and set it in the area where the students practiced the program. They sat on chairs, looking at the sleigh.

"Are you and the students getting excited?"

"We are a production from their creativity, with a little help from some appropriate songs."

"Switching subjects, our wedding, I'm helping you a lot, and I like that. I have a lot of say in what's happening, a lot of my ideas. I like that, Tess."

He touched her cheek and smiled.

"Yeah, dude, guys often get left out of the planning. You're handling so much, 'cause school for me."

"Is over-the-top with all that you have to do. I'm having fun working through the wedding, the reception, and your move into my home after the new year."

"Beth and I talk about it a little; she mentions another home, once in a while. She'll really just remember this home when she gets older."

"Our prenuptial meetings with the lawyers, and with reverend, there're on your calendar?"

"Right, and I have my assignment almost completed for reverend."

"I'm finished with my assignment. There are so many questions. We're finding out so much. We do have a few years we've known each other. But this is the gut information, the real us, that's what these assignments are for. We got to really examine ourselves."

"Craig, in order to make this marriage work your lawyer and Granddad Ethan, they're helping us with our prenuptial agreement."

"Right, do you understand why that's so important?"

"Course," she smiled to him, "you own land, a home, a farming business, and what I bring into this marriage is my love for you, and the hope of acceptance of my Beth."

Tess watched Craig's eyes narrow and he shook his head.

"My sister, I'm not sure about her. Dad's lawyer felt that there was an equal distribution because mom had life insurance, a lot of it, and my sister got that. Mom understood how important life insurance would be because she never worked jobs that paid much, so did not have a 401K, and she died years before she could collect social security."

"Coleen was a partner to your dad, in everything they did on the land, and with the home, real life partners. I recognize how important that was to your dad, Craig."

They stood up as Craig gave the sleigh another look, checking its ability to remain upright.

"Wow, I am pleased," she watched his smile and his happy eyes. "I gotta head out; we've accomplished a great deal here, and not just the sleigh. We've got a handle on our futures, doing the preliminary work, which one day we'll thank our lucky stars we did."

"Thank you for everything, Craig, and Granddad Ethan spoke of what you just said, we doing all this for our one day."

They hugged, and Craig caressed her lips with a soft kiss. A shimmer of happiness surrounded her. She helped him carry his equipment from her classroom. The sleigh stood in the corner. Tess smiled as she envisioned her students tomorrow morning. They hugged, and she returned to the classroom.

Tess stood in her orderly organized classroom. She felt her smile widen as she watched the fading light from her windows bring in the last bit of warmth to her room.

"The kids, they're gonna be as happy as I already am. Fun, we will have fun presenting this in celebration of the holiday," she paused, "with the younger students. Thank you, God, for continuing to watch over me, and all of us," she spoke out.

ℰꙮ

Three days before the end of the term, and the Christmas break Tess got to see her dream unfold. The principal decided that an afternoon performance would fit with the academic schedule for Downing. From start to finish the program took 16 minutes.

Tess gathered her 5th graders around her after the show concluded.

"I am so proud of you."

She looked from her actors to the young man draped in burlap, representing the horse. Her eyes went to stage hands and 5th graders who sang the three songs. They dressed all in black. Among them she nodded to the student stage manager and the sound technician, and the student in charge of programs.

"We love you, Miss Palmerst. We had fun, awesome," they all spoke. "Did you hear all the applause, and the audience laughing?"

Tess burst into tears, her throat so constricted she could not speak. She nodded to them. She held her hand over her throat and finally she gasped, "I did."

The students cleared the stage, set the sleigh back in the corner for Craig to take apart during the holiday break, and put away the sound system. Following her signal the group did a quiet walk back to their classroom. When they all got inside, everyone jumped up and down. They kept their soft voices as they celebrated. One of the parents left snacks of brownies and pop for the group.

"We're all hungry, after all that," Stephanie spoke out to the other students.

They sat at their desks; some put their heads down. Tess saw the relief in their eyes.

Later she got a call from Craig.

"It was wonderful, Tess, job well done."

"Gosh, you were there, Craig?"

"Yeah in the back; I knew you would never see me. You do so great with your kids. But I wanted to let you know."

"Thanks, the students liked it, that's what matters."

℘

Two days later the semester ended. Students hugged Tess as they left for the holiday break. About half the class shared they would come to her wedding and the reception. Three mothers indicated they would each drive a group of students to the church and other parents would pick students up at the reception.

Beth and Tess talked to each other about becoming a part of a bigger family, with Craig.

"You wuv him, Mommy."

"I do. I'm pleased you can see that."

"And, Mommy, Craig woves me, he tol me."

℘

"I love you, sweet girl."

"And I love you, Dad."

"You're stunning, in your beautiful gown, and the flowers in your hair, perfect."

Tess waited for a moment until the song began. A white-lit tree stood to the right of the altar, and red poinsettias graced the back of the altar and the floor around the altar. She saw a single red rose lying on the altar surface.

She held a single red rose as she moved forward to Craig.

Joe kissed Tess on the cheek and guided her to him.

"In love's embrace, there's life's deepest joy."

Tess and Craig spoke that to each other.

"Encouragement, honor, understanding, believing in each other," they shared that along with the words of the wedding vows and prayers to God and the Great Spirit.

They kissed and hugged each other. She turned to Craig. He nodded, smiled, and they walked hand in hand down the aisle. Her students could not help it. Tess watched them, smiling as they stood and clapped and clapped for Craig and her. She watched their smiles as several of the girls jumped up and down.

"Happy, they are happy as we are," she smiled and nodded as they passed other guests.

Family and friends moved next door to the church community room. Everyone got to hear Christmas music with her students singing "Christmas Bells" to the two of them. After that the DJ played lively dance music. At the first dance Tess waltzed with her dad. Craig's dad suggested he dance with his sister.

"We honor Mom," Craig whispered to Jill.

"We do; I am happy for you, Craig. Tess already seems like such a sister to me. She's reached out, especially with the boys."

"I'm glad, Jill. Her students love her, as you saw when they sang to us."

Several of Craig's family came from the reservation. They brought the flute player who helped at Coleen's funeral reception. The gathering stayed silent as the performer shared the words of a wedding song which he then played. Craig and Tess held hands through the song, giving each other a kiss as the flutist neared the song's finish.

Granddad Ethan stood back and watched everyone.

"Marvelous, what a mix of folks, little children, folks from the Apsaalooke area where they live, the families and friends of mainly Craig, and the few of us for Tess. Yeah, it was best that Beth not be included. She would remember none of this."

Emily came to him, "So much fun, could I invite you out for a dance while the DJ is still doing some fast stuff?"

Ethan and Emily danced, staying together for two dances. Craig and Tess passed by them, at the second swing dance.

"Having fun?" Tess spoke out in passing

"Yes," Ethan and Emily smiled and spoke in unison.

Craig and Tess separated and spoke to as many of the guests as they could. Her students gathered near her as they got ready to leave and moved into a big group hug.

"Merry Christmas, Miss Palmerst, tell your husband for us. And what is your new name again?"

"Huntcrowe," she spelled it out for them. "There's that e at the end of the name."

"And Happy New Year to all of you. Thank you so much for coming."

The last student who left her spoke out, "We love you, Mrs. Huntcrowe, see you soon."

Tess kept smiling and thanking guests for coming, this very busy time of year. She found a table near the back of the group. She stood for a moment before she approached them.

"Dad, with Granddad Ethan on one side of him, and Granddad Jack, on his other side," she whispered, "I did not ever think that would happen, those three men, together. Grandma Donna, you're looking down at us. See how it's all worked out?"

She gave a tiny nod of her head and moved toward them. All three men stood and clapped for her.

"Donna, your granddaughter, what a beautiful woman, with her long white gown and a circle of greenery and roses in her hair," Granddad Ethan thought.

"I'm clapping for you three now," Tess began clapping as they stopped. "Thank you so much, for coming to see Craig and me begin our lives together."

"You are correct, Tess," her dad spoke up, "this is the beginning of your lives together. We will be with you two, and Beth, for all our lives, agreed, gentlemen?" he turned and looked at Granddad Jack, and then at Granddad Ethan.

"We agree, be here for you," Ethan and Jack spoke and nodded to Tess.

As the crowd thinned, Craig and Tess went to the table where Craig's dad and his sister and family sat.

"Brent, thank you, Jill and Ted and kids, I'm so glad you all could come on this day after Christmas."

Brent and Jill stood and moved around to the couple. They all hugged. Craig shook hands with Ted across the table. The boys waved to him.

"We'll be going, but we look forward to the next years with all of you," Jill said as she smiled to Craig and Tess.

ॐ

"Were you glad we had a photographer?"

"Oh, my yes, Craig, that was so important, and you thought of it. And to have cupcakes for a wedding cake, the bakery did a super job, with white, chocolate, and carrot as options. Our guests sure enjoyed those."

"It turned out," Craig turned and touched her cheek, "oh, wow."

"Yeah, uh huh, totally wow."

They drove into the well-plowed lane to the home.

"Unbelievable, my home now."

"We'll come back to the car for our stuff; I need to carry you over the threshold. You haven't been to the Huntcrowe home very many times."

He picked her up and carried her in.

"Welcome, Mrs. Huntcrowe."

He gave her a soft kiss and she returned his kiss. When he set her down, they hugged, not wanting to leave the embrace. They both cried.

"For so long, my hope, my desire for you, Tess."

"Your patience, your love for me."

They stood together, holding on until their tears lessened.

"Wow, the emotion of all this," she whispered to him.

He kissed her on the forehead. Then they brought in the cupcakes and other loads and set everything in the kitchen.

"Aunt Emily is bringing the presents tomorrow. We've got a couple of big days coming up."

"For sure, Tess, and thank you for helping me decide that spring break week would be the best time for a short honeymoon."

They kissed and kissed. The intense pressure in her groin area kicked in her arousal. He took her hand and guided her to the bedroom they would now share. Tess looked around at this quiet room with its natural lighting shining in. She turned and saw the bed. A single red rose lay in the middle.

"Oh Craig," she choked out the words and pointed to the rose, "our love, bright like this rose, thank you."

"I love you, Tess."

"And I love you."

They undressed in front of each other, Craig helping her with the zipper on the back of her white gown. They lay, coming together almost immediately, exploding into each other. After that they lay entwined for a few minutes, kissing and caressing. Again they became one, in the quiet of their room. In the afterglow of their lovemaking they rested in each other's arms. This late afternoon brought a magnificent sunset, which they saw out of the southwest side of the bedroom window.

"Red, almost the color of the rose, and pink, and lavender; oh Tess, the sunset, our gift from God, for our magnificent late wedding afternoon."

"God blesses us," she whispered and then kissed him.

They dressed in jeans and sweatshirts. Tess remembered her blue jeans and her Downing sweatshirt. They padded in bare feet to the kitchen, holding hands.

She fixed scrambled eggs, bacon, and cupcakes. Craig opened a bottle of champagne and they talked and talked, about the wedding, all the different guests each of them saw.

"Your students, my, it's something to be around young people. Some of them are so grown up. I noticed the boys who came, they were tiny, compared to the girls, who seemed much more mature."

"The kids, they definitely made the wedding reception interesting. I am so happy I insisted on no alcohol, with students there."

"I agree, and the dancing, that was so much fun."

"I loved the dance where all my students and I stood together, holding hands in a circle, and swaying back and forth, even the boys; I saw smiles."

Tess shook her head as they finished their meal, "You know, Craig, you and I never had been to a dance together. Had we ever really danced before?"

"I can't recall; there were several years where we just saw each other, like in bits and pieces."

"You're right. Hey, dude, we have a very incredible week coming up, leading to New Year's Eve."

"Tess, I'm super glad we are doing a quiet time that eve. I absolutely hate to be out on the roads, and having guests drive away, oh yuk."

"Absolutely, quiet, that's us."

"Beth joins us tomorrow. I'll be her dad."

Tess watched his smile and the shine in his eyes.

"This is meant to be," she thought, and nodded as she thought of her grandma and her folks.

"Talking to Grandma Donna?"

"Yeah, and to my mom, and dad."

∽

"I want to remember each day of this transition of my life," Tess spoke out the next morning as she kissed Craig.

They would all meet up at her apartment in an hour.

Beth ran to her as Tess entered Aunt Em's.

"I missed you, Beth."

"Missed you, Mommy, Aunt Em, heped me."

"As she always does."

"Marry, you, daddy?"

"Yes, your daddy and I married. And now we have you, our precious daughter, to begin our lives together, the three of us."

"Happy?"

"Oh, Beth, I am so happy. I want you to be happy too."

Tess watched her daughter smile to her and nod her head, "Yes, happy."

"Ready to move to your new home, Beth?"

"Reay."

∽

Tess stayed up most of one night before the wedding preparing for the move from her apartment.

"I am so glad I'm organized," she told Beth as they walked through the apartment where they lived these past months. A half hour later two pickups drove up to move them to the Huntcrowe home. Tess downsized, giving away the couch and chair to a nonprofit. She first asked Emily if that would be OK. Emily agreed that she didn't need the old furniture back. A newly organized church took Tess's little dining room table and chairs for the kitchen area in the church.

The attitude Tess always had, growing up with just essentials, was "If it's not important to my living, then someone else really needs the stuff."

She continued to feel that way now and tried to say each day, "I am so blessed."

Beth's bed and furniture remained the whole family's top priority in the move. Once her bed, bookcase and books, and her toy box got moved in, Beth helped make her own bed.

"Whatcha think about your curtains?" Granddad Joe asked.

"Baby blue, buful," she smiled and hugged him.

"I knew you'd like them. I checked with your mom, found them and hung them up for you.

Thank you, Gran Joe."

He helped her finish making her bed. They took the frame with the words Beth nearly memorized.

"Where do you want the poem, Beth?"

"Peez, on my wall, up there, Muth Teres."

"Like this poem?"

She nodded to Granddad Joe, "Give best anway."

"You read this with your mom, every night?"

"Ever night," Beth smiled, "for bed."

She took his hand and walked him out of her room. She stopped and peeked back in.

"Own room."

"Yes Beth, very nice."

Joe saw her smile and the shine in her greenish blue eyes.

That late afternoon Grandma Marty brought a picnic meal for the moving helpers at the Huntcrowe home.

"We got maybe a half hour left of putting Tess's things away. She's got everything figured out."

The crew sat on the rug in the great room. Tess watched the gas-lite fire cheering the helpers. Out the windows she watched the wind begin to shake the bare trees. They chowed down on chicken breasts and wings, potato salad, baked beans, carrots and broccoli, and the final cupcakes from the wedding.

"Dewishous," Beth spoke out.

"That's for sure, granddaughter, your grandma does such fine fried chicken."

The grandparents smiled to each other, a rare occasion when Granddad Joe and Grandma Marty sat close to each other.

"Goodness, they seem happy, guess it's for me, and my family," Tess nodded.

"You're thinkin', sweet girl," Joe smiled to Tess.

"I am, Dad, so happy, Craig, over the moon for him, and our daughter here with us."

"Thank you, Marty, for this. I guess you know how this bunch likes to eat," Brent added.

"I do, and I hope this is the beginning of meals this family will have together, over the next years. For sure, Craig and Tess have drawn us closer together."

"Wonderful meals and times together, Mom," Tess nodded and smiled to her mom.

ഇ

During the summer of 2005 Craig forged ahead with his plan. By the start of the school year, before harvest, he became Beth's adopted father.

"It's what I've wanted to do all along, since almost the first time I met this precious little girl."

He shared that with family and friends, and with Bobby John, Beth's biological father. Bobby John agreed, asking only for a picture of Beth and a card at Christmas. Both Tess and Craig agreed that one day, far in the future, they might tell Beth about her biological dad. And they made that agreement because of what happened to Tess's Granddad Evan.

Beth knew her alphabet and started printing it out. She loved doing her full name, Beth Ann Huntcrowe.

"Name now Huntcrowe. Daddy adop me."

Tess heard the pride in her daughter's voice as she shared that with folks and brought her latest artwork, with her name at the top.

&

"I don't know for sure, and I want you to know, Craig, I think we're having a baby, looks like next May."

They stood together on the back patio, gazing at the sunset. He turned to her and kissed her, a long sensual kiss. They put their arms around each other and held on for a long time. She felt the pound, pound of his heart, and of hers.

"Our dream, going to be fulfilled, oh Tess, wonderful."

"I don't want to say anything, until we're for sure. I've missed two periods and the test I took myself showed positive."

They made love that night, in the quiet glow of moonlight splashing across their bedroom.

"My beloved, Craig, our tomorrows, so clear to me, the four of us, Beth, the little one, you and me."

"Beyond what I could ever have imagined, sweetheart."

They said a prayer together, a prayer for family, as they drifted off to sleep in each other's arms.

In early October Tess began to sense something different about her body. The tiredness of being pregnant seemed ever present. They still had not shared with family about her condition. It was a Thursday afternoon after her students left. She stood in the middle of her classroom and remembered Donna.

"What's up, Grandma? Not sure why I'm thinkin' of you. I don't feel good, not like me, I'm young, got lots of energy, or did have. I'll get Beth, then drop by Aunt Em's. I really need to talk to her. And stay with me, I think I'm gonna need you, keep talkin' to you."

The three of them sat at Em's kitchen island. Beth drew pictures, of her farmhouse and of the barn in back. She used her thin-tipped special markers she kept at Aunt Em's.

"You don't look well, Tess, lots going on?" Aunt Em asked her niece.

She watched Tess, her forehead furrowing and a fog in her usually bright eyes.

"You're right, I'm not sure, stressed," she shook her head, "don't know why."

Tess felt a painful jolt in her groin area. She excused herself to the bathroom. As she sat on the stool she felt another sharpness as a gush of blood smacked into the stool. Another cramp and another gush, "I know what this is, I'm expelling the fetus," she spoke out.

She took deep breaths as the pain subsided for a short time.

"Aunt Em, Aunt Em," Tess shouted as she stood and moved to the door, a towel pressed against further bleeding. "I need you, in the bathroom."

Emily peeked in, saw her niece's face, "You're losing the babe."

Tess nodded, "I can make it to the Emergency Room, get my coat, help Beth with her coat, and grab our bags."

Tess let Beth sit on her knees as the nurse wheeled them into the ER.

Within the hour Tess lay on the operating table, ready for the D & C.

"I'll be OK, Craig's coming for Beth. She knows I'll be home in a day. Aunt Em has my bag to give to Craig, and Beth has her backpack. God, watch over me and all of mine, please," she whispered.

"Ready for sleep?" she heard a male voice, then a different male voice, "the docs," she nodded.

"I am, thanks for getting me in so quick. Need to get back to my students, to my husband and daughter."

She opened her eyes and saw his face, smiling to her. She smiled back.

"Awesome to see you, Craig. Docs got me fixed up?"

"They did; you came through the procedure just fine."

"Beth?"

"Aunt Em's spending the night at our home. She'll take Beth to child care before she heads for school. She's talked to your principal and taken care of the substitute for you. The principal insists that the sub be on board for tomorrow, Friday, and at least Monday, Tuesday, and Wednesday of next week. I asked the docs, they think you'll be ready for your students by that time. You are just so young, with that first baby at 16."

"Thank you, Craig, for everything. I'm in shock, still haven't had a chance to realize what's happened. Again, I'm so glad we didn't share with anyone. Miscarriages happen, that's for sure."

"We'll grieve, I want us to see a grief counselor, when you're ready."

"Our child is with God, in God's hands, being loved and loving, in that tiny little form."

Craig moved into the hospital bed with Tess. He kissed her cheek.   They cried together, verbalizing how much they wanted this child, conceived in their love for each other.

They ate a very late meal together in her room. She had a light meal, eggs, toast, and hot tea which tasted good to her. Craig ordered a hamburger and fries. They shared chocolate ice cream.

"Heading out, your eyes are way bright, the drugs."

"I'll sleep, try at least, God's with me, I just gotta float along in His hands for now."

"I love you, Tess."

"And I love you, Craig."

"We have all our tomorrows," he smiled to her and kissed her forehead.

He watched her close her eyes, smiling up to him.

&

Tess felt a hollowness in her mind and her whole body. And she cried almost all the time. On Tuesday of the next week she insisted on going back to her students, that being with them was the answer to returning to her old self. It helped to be back in her classroom, a familiarity which she cherished.

Craig and Aunt Em continued to watch over her. Tess ate very little, read to Beth, and as soon as her daughter went to bed she lay down.

"I'm so sad," she whispered to her husband whenever they were together without Beth. "I've lost my will to try, my mind, it's numb."

Craig kept up the home, laundry, meals and Beth's care. Emily brought their minister out for coffee and dessert on Wednesday evening. Tess sat with them, before the warm fire. But she did not contribute, and after dessert Craig, Emily and the minister left the fireplace area. By then Tess had her head in her hands, tears starting again.

"She needs more help than we can give here. I've worked with our family doctor, and her ob/gyn."

"I agree, the minister shared, "she's having a postpartum kind of depression, with the loss of the fetus also. Craig, Springbright is a good facility; she needs to rest, with her not sleeping. And she needs to start talking about herself; she's pushed herself so hard for these past few years. I even saw that in church choir, her joyful participation."

Emily saw Craig's tears as they stood with quiet talk in the kitchen.

"There's a beautiful fire, family near, yet she doesn't see or feel any of what is happening. We must bring her back."

"Yes, Craig, we must."

"I've lost this child; I gotta go on, so she can heal and go on. She's not mentioned a word about God, or about His will for her. But I know what I must do. What now, my will must be strong. God's at my side."

That thought circled in his head. The three of them came into a hug. Emily left, but not before whispering to Craig, "Whatever I can do; I want to help."

"Thank you, angel from God."

Emily smiled and glanced at Tess.

"God bless and keep this family," she whispered as she drove back to town.

&

Craig woke with a start. He checked the clock, 3 a.m. He moved to Tess. She was not in their bed. He threw on a shirt and looked around their room. A slab of moonlight lightened one corner. He checked on Beth, sound asleep. With his flashlight he went through the house, listening for her, for her crying.

Silence, he heard that everywhere he turned. His stomach cramped and sweat stood on his forehead.

"God, help me find her. I pray she did not go outside."

He looked in the garage, both cars inside.

His tears began, "God, I'm gonna lose it, help me, oh help me."

Then he noticed it, the door to the basement, usually closed, was open a tiny crack. He started down the steps, then stopped and listened. He heard it, a faint cry, then harder crying. He moved the flashlight around.

"Craig, oh Craig, you found me."

He moved to the huddled figure, sitting in front of the dryer with clothes piled around her. He helped her stand up. They hugged as he told her, "I love you, Tess, I love you."

&

"Mrs. Huntcrowe, you were really sick. We're so glad you're better."

"Thanks, Angie, and thank you class for your card, and for moving forward with your studies. I owe you an explanation. All of us suffer loss, like Trent's telling us when his grandma died."

Several other students shared losses they had.

"And I had a loss, that is, my husband and I did. I lost our baby, very early in its life. I got so sad about the loss, because

I've never really had a loss in a long time. It hit me hard. I got help, that's why I've been gone."

"We are sorry, Mrs. Huntcrowe."

"Thank you, and the best thing for all of us is to work hard together."

"And Christmas is coming," a student added.

"Wow, yes, that's going to be wonderful for all of us."

ℬ

Craig sat with Emily in the little café where the family sometimes had lunch in Beet City. Brent joined them as they got their coffee on that Saturday afternoon.

"How can I ever thank you for helping with Tess? The important thing is that she's back with her students, and responding really good to Beth. I guess we all just lost about three and a half weeks of this fall season."

"No thanks needed, Craig, and it wasn't a loss of time, just time helping," Emily smiled to him.

"And Dad, I couldn't a done it, the end of harvest, the beets, and everything else without your help."

"I loved being back on the farm, being in charge part of the time. I wouldn't want to try it again, but it was really good for me to be with you. Support you gave me when we were losing your mother, never'll forget that."

Brent looked, first into Craig's eyes and then into Emily's, "She off the meds?"

"Pretty much, what she says is that she's got her right mind back."

"She's bounced back remarkably well," Brent nodded to them.

"Yup, can tell you I thought for a while I was going to lose her. And then I got so angry, at God, and how could he do this to our remarkable family. But our minister helped me through my black mood times."

Craig felt salty tears come to his eyes, "At times, through all this with Tess I just wanted to walk away from her, from my life, and that's appalling. Truly it's been the biggest crisis of my life."

Craig took a minute to wipe his eyes and nose. He blew out a big breath as he looked at his family.

"We're back to the clean and organized home, Tess helping me with cooking, working with Beth on her reading, and relaxing a little in the evenings. We still read to Beth, and she reads to us. Once we have prayer time with her, she settles down and sleeps. That gives Tess and me time together. We sit in front of the fire and talk a little about our day. One thing for sure, she expresses her gratitude for all of us helping her through the mind-numbing depression."

"We're family, Craig," Brent smiled to his son.

Craig nodded.

6

"We are family," she whispered.

Tess stood in the kitchen as her mind swirled over the past years and times with families and students together and apart. She reminded herself of the students she worked with, during the 2005 and 2006 school years. She saw their faces, first names and when she remembered them most clearly, at holiday times. For this fall of 2007 she worked with students at Downing part time.

She felt surrounded with the warm blanket of Craig's love and her family's caring. Tears came to her eyes, "Oh, Craig, the crushing sadness of losing a baby," she shared with him, not so much now. She remembered that devastating time.

But this boy, he would be a strong addition to the family, his shock of black hair, eyes that would turn brown soon, and tan skin, much darker than his dad's.

"Our son, a glorious miracle in my life, Tess."

She watched the wide smile on his face and the dark shine in his eyes as Craig looked up to her. He sat at the kitchen table giving Tom his bottle.

"And in mine, the miracle, he's growin' so fast."

"Yeah, little ones tend to do that."

"You'll get used to the spurts, wait'l he's 14."

Craig laughed, "No way, I want him to stay small forever."

"It'll never happen, slick," Tess kissed her husband on the top of his head.

"Mommy, guests are coming up the walk."

"Please greet them, sweet girl."

"Going, Mommy."

Tess gazed at her tall dark blonde daughter as she headed for the front door. She smiled down at Craig and their son, the warm glow of her feelings for them wrapping around her, and them.

Folks already said he harkened back to his granddad, Brent, and that whole side of Craig's family. Tess observed that in Thomas John Huntcrowe, his broad forehead and width through his shoulders, already. Beth started calling him TJ soon after he came into the family.

"Tom makes me think of someone older, and I will not have a brother called Tommy," she spoke up. "He's TJ, far's I'm concerned."

This Sunday in July the Huntcrowes declared as their Independence Sunday. It just so happened that some of both sides of the family could be together for a picnic in their backyard. The family sat and stood, gazing out at the field of sugar beets, green and lush.

Craig cooked hamburgers, and family brought all the rest of the fixings. They all got a look at TJ and had pictures taken with him. Tess put him down for his afternoon nap. All ate and ate, and talked and everyone filled everyone else in on what happened with the family. They had not all been together since the previous Christmas, of 2006.

"What for you and your school year coming up, Tess?" Brent asked.

"Sharing an assignment all year, I'm mornings. Beth and I are both at Downing, her for kindergarten and me, with the fifth graders. Craig will take care of TJ. We'll get home from school early afternoon."

"An opportunity to get to know your son?"

"Right, Dad," he smiled to Brent. "He'll be right out there with me mornings as we harvest in the fall. I already have a baby-carrying backpack."

"Then spring semester?" Grandma Marty asked.

"We'll all three head out in the mornings, us to school and TJ to child care. Craig's got planting in the spring. We'll be home afternoons. The big challenge, when Beth's in first grade the next fall.

Beth came and put her arm around her mom's shoulder, "I'll be at the same school as mommy. But I won't see her hardly at all. The big kids, they're in another part of the school, away from us little guys."

"In the spring, besides planting, I'm involved in a Young Farmers group, plus I'm an officer in the Beet Growers Associations for Montana and a couple other states."

"So you'll be away some?"

"I will be, short assignments. And when we're all finished with dessert, I'll give you a tour of something I'm really proud of, a skill I been honing for a time."

৪০

Craig walked with the family to a side part of the barn, a kind of office area that Brent used when he and Coleen took over the farm operation from Brent's dad.

"A couple of commissionings, I call them, got to get one of these out to the res."

"Beautiful wood," Joe touched a tiny corner of the small table surface.

"An entrance table, in the foyer of a home?"

"Right, Marty, I've made three, one's a model for the others. I plan to do just smaller furniture, special pieces, that aren't often found in furniture stores."

"A hobby for you?" Emily asked.

"Yeah, but only a little time out here, when the children and Tess are away. I really like to work with my hands, didn't discover that until a short time ago. Didn't even think about it when I helped build our home. Aunt Lily, she explained what she wanted. Together we drew up the plan."

"Daddy," Beth looked up to her dad, "Can we go look at the cross, show everyone our cathedral in the trees?"

"Course, let me close up here."

Beth led the group down the lane to the road. She stopped where there was a break in the wood fencing. They all walked into the trees and in a few seconds, they stood in front of the cross.

"Daddy showed this to me first in the winter. Snow blew all over the dead tree, and stuck because of the cold. I saw a white cross, with a thick tree branch sticking out of each side. And Daddy, can you say what you say to Mommy and me?"

"Certainly, sweet girl, with the winter sunlight shining down on the snowy cross," Craig moved his arm from the sunlight to the cross, "I say, 'May the light of the love of God bring joy and peace to you and all of yours this Christmas.'"

It was silent as the group gazed at the dead tree.

"Thank you for sharing, Craig and Beth. I'll want to come back to see your cathedral when Christmas arrives," Joe spoke out.

"And some of the rest of us also," Brent added.

&

The families got ready to depart.

"This's a great way to spend a special July day. Thank you Craig and Tess; so much nicer than the Independence Day turmoil we often encounter."

Brent spoke that and the rest of the family agreed. They shared their love and concern for their family and for their country, the US of A.

Tess fed TJ, and Beth and Craig did the little final cleanup. The rest of the family helped earlier.

After they ate a small supper and Beth and TJ had their baths the family sat together out on the patio couch. Tonight Beth read to TJ and her mom and dad. Beth requested *The Wizard of Oz* after she saw the movie with her parents.

"I love being able to read, Mommy and Daddy."

"We know that, your books are good friends, which you always can read 'til you fall asleep."

Craig said goodnight to Beth and peeked in to see that TJ's eyes closed. He stepped into their bedroom. Tess greeted him with her pink nightie on.

"Sweetheart, it's been so long."

"Seems like many years, but I'm healed."

They nestled in each other's arms. Their want for each other peaked as they breathed hard, coming together with the glorious burst of their climaxes.

℘

"It's a superior idea to celebrate Thanksgiving on the Saturday after the date, two days later. We're combining baptisms from earlier this morning and a meal of thankfulness." Brent spoke out as he stood looking around at the seated family in the Craig Huntcrowe home.

"The baptisms, so meaningful with our family and godparents, Aunt Emily, and Ted."

"Hear, hear," Jack spoke out, "for our darling little ones, Beth and TJ."

"Thank you, Emily and Ted, for offering to be godparents," Craig nodded to each of them in turn.

"I'm with God, and today I'm dedicated to God. That's my baptism."

Beth smiled to her parents and nodded, "Like Mommy and Daddy say, God, He is with me always."

"That's right, sweet granddaughter."

The family held hands and said silent grace.

They ate and talked and laughed together. Craig got up with Tess as they each took an empty dish to fill up from the stove. They stood together, then turned to each other. Their lips touched, feeling the softness of their kiss. They refilled the dishes and moved away from the stove, gazing out at their family. Then they turned, looking out the kitchen window, looking over the land, the beet fields in the distance.

Craig whispered in her ear, "Our love, this land, and our family, close with us."

"As I always hope it shall be," Tess looked up to him and smiled.

A Voice for Gabby

Almost 15-year-old Gabby survives an explosion which takes the lives of her teammates and her spirit team sponsor. Her brain injury leaves her without memory or the ability to speak. Gabby's dad helps with her educational rehabilitation through the summer after the accident. She decides she will work hard to represent her former team by being a good student.

Her neighbor, Josh, comes back into her life. He and his sister played with Gabby when they were younger. Josh's affection for Gabby grows as he spends time with her. Her parents and Josh support her as she progresses through relearning how to read. She must also review eight years of schooling, for which she has no memory.

Still unable to speak Gabby retakes ninth grade at Hillyer, a school better suited to her educational situation. She discovers she can dance and has gymnastics ability learned over past years. Dancing brings her happiness, and she hopes that somehow she may start to regain other parts of her memory.

Josh and Gabby now attend the same school. Their friendship grows. Gabby discovers sexual feelings in herself and for Josh. Her mom gives her a book explaining what is going on with her body. Gabby does well at Hillyer and begins to feel she is catching up in her studies, except in English. Spelling and writing essays continue to be difficult for her. Her English teacher suggests books she needs to read over the summer before her sophomore year. A part time job and reading books keep her busy. She passes both her written and practical driving exams and becomes a cautious driver.

Josh suffers serious injuries while riding his bike. Gabby spends time with him through his hospitalization and rehabilitation. She loves him, as he loves her. Gabby joins a new spirit team at Hillyer. Dancing brings her joy. While out riding bikes with Josh as part of his rehab, she speaks two words. With speech therapy she begins to regain her voice, from a loud soprano in the past to a soft, scratchy alto now. At the first fall pep assembly she dances with the new spirit team. As she performs, she feels a bright light surrounding her. She remembers again what a miracle she is.

About Cathleen

www.CathleenEllis.com

Cathleen Ellis is a Colorado native. She and her husband, John, live in the northern part of the state. They have four sons, three daughters-in-law, and four grandchildren. Cathleen draws the inspiration for her love stories from the lives of young people with whom she has lived and worked her entire life.